ONE TWISTED GAME

JESSICA LYNN SORENSEN

To my favorite reader,
Enjoy the ride!!

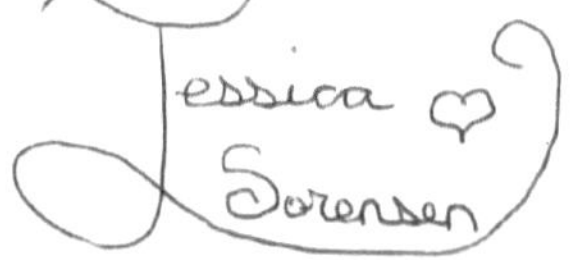

ONE TWISTED GAME

PROLOGUE

My mind blanks as I cross the threshold. I don't remember opening the door. One moment I'm pressed against the hallway's cold wall, sweat slicking my fingertips, heart hammering against bone as if begging to escape, and the next, I'm inside looking at the man who has haunted my nightmares and thoughts for years.

There he stands.

My brother.

The brother whose name Mom couldn't say without her voice shattering. The brother whose bedroom became a shrine we all avoided. The one who looked up to me.

He looms by the towering window, his silhouette etched against a trembling halo of light. Dust motes drift like trapped embers. For a second, he looks both impossibly close and a lifetime away. His shoulders are squared but relaxed, as if he's bracing himself for something he's been expecting all along. One hand drifts to the small of his wife's back. The gesture is small but achingly intimate... an anchor in a room full of past ghosts.

She's radiant in a way that makes the air feel warmer. Her skin is flushed, and hair is loose, curling around her temples. The dark circles beneath her eyes speak of sleepless nights and growing pains. There's a steadiness in her touch, a quiet fierceness that roots him to the ground. She's the calm center of his storm. Her belly arches forward, taut and full, the promise of life pressing gently against the fabric of her dress.

When she meets his gaze, her eyes brush over him like a soothing wind, smoothing every sharp corner in the space between them. The love between them hums, low and constant, a pulse that steadies even as the rest of us begin to unravel, choking on memories we've spent years trying to hold on to.

The whole room seems to breathe with him, like the walls themselves remember the boy he was before the world tore him away. Before we stopped setting his place at dinner. Before the police let his case go cold.

I can almost feel the hush that falls between us. It's the kind of silence that carries weight, a silence made of things we never said and things we're terrified to say now.

He swivels toward us. His gaze drifts from Mom's trembling lips to Dad's taut shoulders, to Nicole's reddened eyes, and finally lands on me. No confusion, only the wary vigilance of someone awakening from too-long a nightmare. I recognize that look. I've seen it on myself a few times.

We freeze. Thirty years of silence press down on us like a suffocating weight. The air thickens in my throat, each breath a jagged shard of memory piercing my lungs.

Mom steps toward him. Her voice cracks open the silence like splintered glass. "Hi, sweetheart."

Lee's eyes flicker. His Adam's apple jerks, but no sound comes. Three decades of absence have welded shut his voice.

Dad clears his throat, gaze pinned to the scuffed floor. "We... we hope we're not overwhelming you." Every word drips with regret, clinging to him like the acrid smoke after a house fire. His hands curl into fists at his sides, knuckles chalk white, as if he's trying to push the years of apologies back into his heart.

He can't bring himself to meet the eyes of the son he failed to protect.

Lee stands rigid, but I see the tremor in his jaw, the quiver of his fingers resting on his wife's shoulder.

"I'm Roger," Dad rasps at last, offering a hand that quivers like a flag in the wind. "Your father."

Lee's fingers close around his palm with the desperation of

a drowning man clutching driftwood. Time stretches between them, a brittle thread strung taut with unspoken sorrow and aching hope.

Mom steps forward, her legs threatening to give way. She lays a trembling hand on Lee's arm. "I'm Nancy." Her voice cracks like old plaster. "Your mom." Her shoulders heave once, a stifled sob caught somewhere between relief and heartbreak floats from her mouth.

Nicole edges in between them, her eyes rimmed in pink from crying earlier. "I'm Nicole," she whispers, her voice catching on the last syllable. "Your big sister." She offers a trembling smile. Her lips quiver, trying to hold it together, but the moment he looks at her, she breaks a little. She presses a knuckle to her mouth, like she can physically hold in the years of grief she swallowed for him.

My throat tightens at the sight.

Lee's lips curl into a fragile, uncertain grin.

And then it's my turn.

Oh, hell, I feel like I'm going to be sick or faint.

His face... God, his face. It's Dad's jawline with Mom's eyes. He still has the little scar near his eyebrow from when he fell into the coffee table.

Say something.

Don't just stand there looking like an idiot.

This is Dustin, for fuck's sake.

"I'm Caleb," I whisper. "Your..." The words die on my tongue. My ribs ache, a dull, constant throb as if my chest cavity can't hold the weight of all the years I spent searching. I'm drowning in all the words I've rehearsed a thousand times.

Lee inhales so sharply I swear I hear his heart stutter. He stares at me, eyes a storm of disbelief and desperation, tear pools trembling at the brim. "Yeah," he mumbles, like he's testing the edges of a dream. "So I heard."

His wife brings a trembling hand to his forehead, smoothing back a stray lock of hair. "It's okay," she whispers. "You don't have to say anything. Just let it come."

Nicole moves again, cradling something in her arms: a battered photo album whose leather cover smells of old glue and dust. Her fingers trace the spine like she's touching an old wound she's afraid to reopen.

She hands it to him without a word.

Lee opens it as though it might shatter. Page after page: Polaroid snapshots of backyard birthdays, summer barbecues, fallen leaves swirling around tiny feet. Scrawled captions in our mother's handwriting. There we are... kids chasing each other across grass, chocolate smeared on our cheeks, our hands intertwined on the old swing set. Each caption, a heartbeat from a life ripped away.

His breath catches; his chest convulses. He turns another page, then another, fingers trembling so violently the photos rattle. Each image strikes like lightning... half memory, half revelation, and I can see it ripping through him. A soft, strangled noise escapes him... half gasp, half sob. His knees give way, and he slides to the floor as his wife catches him.

"No..." he sighs, his voice cracking open. "No... oh God..."

His eyes glaze over. "These were in my dreams," he chokes out. "Your faces... I thought they were nightmares." He presses a shaking hand to his heart. "They were memories."

And then he crumples into sobs that come not from his throat but from some hollow place deep inside him. It's the kind of grief you can feel in your bones.

Nicole collapses beside him. Mom kneels too, her hands cupping his face, soft as moth wings. "My sweet boy," she says.

Dad stands a moment longer, tears rolling down his cheeks in silent rivulets. His shoulders quake, the years of regret finally cracking open beneath the weight of forgiveness he doesn't think he deserves.

I fall to my knees beside Lee. He reaches blindly for me,

gripping my arm like the only solid thing left in the world.

"Caleb," he whispers, his voice like sandpaper against silk. "I remember you." He nods against my shoulder, his breathing ragged, each exhale hot through my cotton shirt. "They took me," he says, his voice cracking on the last word. "I don't know how to..."

"It's okay," I tell him, though nothing about this will ever be okay. "You don't have to. Not now."

My hand cups the back of his head, and the second he leans into the touch, I break. Silent tears spill down my face, falling onto the album, onto the childhood we both lost.

We stay like that on the floor, the album splayed open between us. Light from the window cuts across our faces, illuminating the wet tracks on his cheeks, the trembling of his hands as they clutch at my shirt like I might disappear from his life again. In that light, I see the boy he once was flicker through the man he's become... a ghost returning to flesh.

Thirty years of searching, and now that I've found him, I realize I've lost him again in ways no reunion can heal. This is more than a meeting of brothers. It's a resurrection of hope from the ashes of every night he was gone.

It isn't the end of our story. Far from it. It's only the first breath of our second chance together.

CHAPTER 1

CALEB

It's been sixteen days since I stood face-to-face with my brother for the first time. Sixteen emotional days. I repeat that number like a spell I'm trying to force into reality, hoping its weight will finally settle somewhere solid inside me. But the memory still floats above me, like a helium balloon caught in some stubborn draft I can't quite pin down.

Two weeks since our hands had touched in that hesitant, unsure grasp. Two weeks since I had watched recognition flicker in his eyes, thin as a match-strike, followed instantly by disbelief. We've only spoken twice on the phone since then, and yet even those brief calls feel richer than anything I ever let myself hope for.

Lee lives across the border in British Columbia, four hours of highway twisting through mountain passes and endless evergreen walls. Geographically close... emotionally, a world apart. He's lived his whole life with that hollow ache of not knowing who he came from.

Our second call stretched over two hours... not because we had endless stories to spill but because neither of us trusted that once we said goodbye, this fragile thread between us wouldn't snap. I kept thinking, *Don't hang up first.*

He told me about his wife, Lexy. Her soft laughter kept drifting through the phone like she was trying to reassure both of us. She's pregnant with twins, a boy and a girl. He plans to name his son Dustin, after the family he never knew.

Us.

He's keeping the name Lee. I understand that. It's all he's ever known. Some things can't be forced, and this is like slowly thawing ice. You can't force someone to thaw all at once.

That same call brought out the fragments he could recall from the day he was taken. I think about it every night before I fall asleep. He said Nicole and I were teasing each other, when a smiling woman appeared, offering to show him the real Batman. He was four, almost five, with wide-eyed wonder. Of course he wanted to go.

What boy wouldn't?

Two other boys trailed her, one barely older than him.

That's what made her seem safe. Harmless.

And that's what twists my stomach into knots. Because this world teaches us to fear the strange man, the candy-offering stranger, the unmarked van lurking too long near the curb. Maybe at best, a half-hearted warning about a suspicious woman. But a mother with children? Society practically pushes lost kids toward her.

"If you're lost, find a mom."

"If you're scared, look for a woman."

"Run to other kids."

So, no, I don't blame him. Not for a second. He did exactly what the world told him to do. He wanted to see Batman, and she promised to bring him right back. She might've even said those exact words... at least, that is what she said in his nightmares.

It has to be real. Parts of it. It lines up with what that guy said about his mother abducting him. We're working on finding her, tracking her down. If we do, we'll age her back a decade or so, and show Lee pictures. See if he recognizes her face.

I know this is hard on all of us. My parents especially. But I can't imagine what he went through. I can't imagine what his parents are feeling right now. I guess it's not that different from what Cassidy's parents went through, thinking they were adopting a child, when really… they were raising someone else's stolen daughter.

I never imagined I'd be engaged to someone whose trauma mirrors my brother's. Never imagined that the connection between two people I care about so fiercely would be built on something so devastating.

And now, the weird symmetry continues. I got left before the wedding with my first fiancée, Samantha. So did he. Lee's version of Samantha was a woman named Amy. Different circumstances, different reasons, but the same wound. It's eerie how our lives kept echoing each other's across miles and years we didn't even know we shared.

Lexy reminds me of Cassidy in small ways: the waxy blonde hair that catches the sun, the curve of her smile when she looks at Lee. The same adoration I see reflecting in Cassidy's eyes when she glances at me.

I haven't reached out to Lee's adoptive parents yet. I don't know if I'm ready. My focus right now is him… building this brotherhood from the ground up, helping him uncover the truth beneath decades of someone else's version of his life.

Two weeks isn't long, but it's enough to know I want more time. So we've postponed the wedding. There's too much unearthing happening for both of us, too much rebuilding to rush past.

And Merrick... God. I still can't look him in the eye. Our conversations have shrunk to short, clipped texts... messages that linger with guilt and unspoken anguish. I nearly sent him to an early grave; I will never forgive myself for that, though I'm grateful the bullet misfired. Luck shouldn't be the only reason your friend is alive.

Chief Reynolds put me on leave, with the condition that I attend therapy and teach a seminar on my first high-profile case. It'll be streamed to every law-enforcement academy, college, and training center across North America. We're going to expose everything—the predators behind Cassidy's abduction, Lee's kidnapping, Cassidy's brother Reid's disappearance, and the six children involved in the case I'll be presenting. Their story is... something else. Unique. Horrific in ways that never leave your mind.

Among the individuals who have discovered who they truly are, the ones reunited with lives they never knew existed, are Phoenix and Zyler Dixon, and Blake Caldwell. Triplets who were taken at birth and adopted out to different families.

Because of cases like theirs, adoption agencies are tightening protocols, rebuilding their licensing process, brick by bureaucratic brick.

We will end this shit, once and for all.

Right now, I'm stepping into my first therapy session, ready to let the broken pieces finally fall where they may.

CHAPTER 2

CALEB

I sit in the lobby stirring the frayed edges of my nerves. Cassidy's voice from the phone call loops through my mind like a broken record.

"Good luck today," she'd said softly over the phone. "I'm proud of you, babe. I love you."

I told her I loved her too, but the instant I hung up, my throat constricted as if coated in gravel. Right now I don't feel like someone worthy of her pride. Or her love. I feel like a house built on sand, leaning in every direction but stable. I feel that if she pushed one fingertip against me, I'd collapse.

Dr. Wagman's door swings open. She's in her mid-fifties, silvering hair pinned back, eyes calm as a still lake. I follow her into the room, my boots sinking into a plush carpet that mocks my unease. She radiates a quiet kind of calm that makes you feel like she's seen worse and won't flinch no matter what you say.

The office is surprisingly cozy. The air is perfumed with the sweet tang of fresh coffee and warm pastries, as though someone just carried in a box of donuts from the bakery next door. The carpet under my boots is plush and soft. She gestures to a low couch covered in textured cushions. On a wooden table, a porcelain teapot steams beside two mismatched mugs. She pours, steam rising like fragile hope, and I imagine swallowing it whole. When she offers me tea, I shake my head. My refusal feels like a confession of how unworthy I am of warmth.

She perches in a high-backed chair, sets her cup down, and lets the silence settle.

"You're Caleb, right?" Her voice is soft but sure, letting the silence stretch like an open door.

"Yeah. Caleb Reed." I tuck my hands between my thighs. My knuckles brush the woven fibers of the couch cushion. I press harder than necessary, hoping physical pressure might hold me together.

She doesn't pick up a clipboard or scribble on paper. She simply folds her hands in her lap.

"Hi, Caleb. I'm Shirley Wagman. What brings you in today?"

I draw in a ragged breath. "Technically? Work. The department encourages it, after all the shit I have been through."

My voice sounds too casual. Too defensive. Like I'm trying to minimize the damage.

Fuck! Why did I say shit? So much for sounding professional.

She nods once, kind but unblinking, and I feel her patience as a gentle shove forward.

I scrape my fingers together. "When I was nine, my four-year-old brother Dustin was abducted. We finally located him, and I met him two weeks ago." The words taste bitter. I can't keep my gaze from dropping to a tiny vase of dried flowers on her table. Feels safer than her eyes.

Dr. Wagman's eyebrows lift, then settle as she remains silent, her gaze unwavering.

"I've never said this out loud," I continue, my gaze now fixed on the tiny stain on the floor. "We thought he was dead. And then we found him. Alive! He's married. Living in Canada."

Her eyelids flicker, but her posture doesn't change. Just listens. It makes me feel seen in a way I'm not prepared for.

"I should be happy," I force the words past my lips. "And I am. Relieved. But that's not all."

She leans in. "What else do you feel?" she asks.

The pattern on the carpet blurs as my eyes water, but I blink it back. It takes a minute to get the words out. "Angry," I finally admit, the word burning on my tongue. I rake my fingers through my hair, pressing into my temple as if to ground myself. Heat thrums under my skin like an electric ache. "So fucking angry... sorry, pardon my language, I just wasn't expecting this feeling."

"Angry," she repeats softly. "At whom?"

I trace the seam of the couch with my eyes. "Everyone, I guess. Myself, God, maybe. The world."

She inclines her head, an invitation to keep going. "Can you say more?"

I shift in the chair, trying to settle a body that won't stay still. My gaze darts to the bookshelf lined with psychology books. All their spines stare back like they know exactly how broken I am. "It's like... I see him now. Lee. That's the name he grew up with. To us, he's still Dustin."

Dr. Wagman leans forward just a little, still listening.

"And he was here, you know? Like, physically. But when I looked at him... he felt like a stranger." My voice catches for the first time. "And he's not supposed to be. He is my damn brother."

"How does that make you feel?" she asks.

"I thought I'd feel joy. Closure. And part of me does. But mostly, I just feel like I was robbed. Like someone tore chapters out of my life. I look at old photos—birthdays, Christmas, just stupid summer stuff, and he's not there. I hate it. I hate knowing he should be next to me, laughing in the sprinkler or stealing my video games."

I feel the weight of the missing years like a hand around my throat, squeezing every time I try to breathe.

"Sometimes," I whisper so low I can barely hear it, "I imagine hurting the people who did this. I want them to feel my pain in their bones."

Dr. Wagman lets the silence settle before she speaks. "Do you feel like something was taken from you?"

I laugh, but it's hollow, stripped of humor. "Yeah. An entire life."

Her eyes hold mine. "And do you know who you're angry at for that?"

My jaw clenches. "The woman who kidnapped him."

"And what do you want to happen to her?"

The words burn as they leave me: "I want her to pay. Dragged out of her hiding place, forced to witness what she stole. I want her to hurt the way we did."

The silence after is so thick I can almost drown in it.

It scares me, the violence inside me, because it's not who I am. It's so powerful it feels like someone else's rage dripping through my veins. Perhaps that someone else is me now. Maybe grief cut me open and rewrote the wiring.

My chest constricts, and I grip the couch cushion to keep me from hyperventilating.

"That's a very human reaction," she says softly, her voice a steady anchor. "You're grieving, Caleb. Anger is part of that process."

I stare at the wall, ashamed to admit what claws at my throat. "But he's not dead," I whisper. Guilt blooms hot in my chest. My loss seems unearned compared to parents who've buried children.

Look at the Fletchers, for example.

She shakes her head gently. "Your loss is real. You lost a version of your brother, of your childhood, of your family. You lost years you'll never get back. Grief shows up whenever something precious is taken."

I bite the inside of my cheek. I stare at the windowpane as rain beads and races downward... each droplet a frantic thought jetting to the finish line. My mind feels just as desperate, jagged fragments clawing for the next spotlight.

Her words land heavier than I expected, like a slow punch to the ribs, because she's right.

She tilts her head and waits. A therapist's silence is louder than a scream. "Is there anything else you wanted to discuss today?"

I nod, drawing in a brittle breath. "My work partner," I begin, opening my mouth to explain, but her eyes flick to the clock.

"Our time is up. We'll start there next session," she says, rising from her chair. "Is that okay?"

I swallow past the lump in my throat. "Yeah. That's okay."

My legs feel like lead. Every confession feels raw and exposed, as though she's peeled back layers of skin to see the blood-pulsing core of me. I can't tell if I'm falling apart or finally coming together.

She pauses at the door, hand on the knob. "One more question... are you angry at your brother?"

Her question slashes through me. I falter, then shake my head. "God, no. He's the only innocent one." A tremor crawls through me. "I'm just devastated I missed so much of his life."

The truth tastes like blood and salt on my tongue.

My heart crushes in my chest. The tears threatening now are of guilt, not anger. The kind that latches on and doesn't let go.

She nods once. "That's an important truth, Caleb. I'm glad you said it."

I feel as if she's reached inside my skull and turned on a light in every dark corner I didn't know existed.

I stand and follow her to the door. I don't say thank you. Not because I'm not grateful, but because I know if I open my mouth, something might break loose that I won't be able to stop.

"Next week?" she asks gently.

I nod in agreement, walking out of the office and into the hallway, feeling heavier and lighter at the same time. Somewhere beneath it all, I think of Cassidy's voice in my ear. *"I'm proud of you."*

CHAPTER 3

CALEB

FOUR DAYS LATER

The rain drums a steady tattoo against the kitchen window, each drop a tiny insistence that the storm still rages outside. Inside, the room feels warm and dim, the overhead light softened by steam swirling from the kettle on the stove. Cassidy's curled on the couch with her legs under a blanket; she watches it with half-focus, her other half trained on me. I can almost see her worry unfurling in the tight grip of her knuckles on the blanket's edge, her restless fingers tracing its frayed seam again and again.

The front door clicks open before Detective Anderson steps in, her dark blazer still speckled with raindrops. She shrugs it off with a deliberate roll of her shoulders, like shedding some invisible burden. The blazer is the same one she always wears when she's carrying bad news... a plain, unadorned black cut that offers no comfort. Her hair's plastered to her forehead, strands stuck from the rain, and she swipes them back with the same distracted motion she uses at crime scenes.

"Hey Darcy, want a drink?" Cassidy's voice is gentle, already on her feet and heading for the counter.

"I'd love one. Make it a double, thanks." Anderson's tone is frayed around the edges. "Just the one, though. I won't be long."

I know that's not true. She promises brevity only when she's braced for a drawn-out confession. The way she avoids my eyes tells me everything I need to know.

I gesture to the armchair across from me; Anderson slides into it with careful hospitality, as if testing the cushion before making herself at home.

Cassidy returns with two glasses of amber liquid, and settles next to me on the couch. One is for herself; the other is for Anderson. Our knees press together against the blanket, and for a moment our fingers brush. A tiny spark of warmth passes between us.

Detective Anderson closes her eyes, breathes in deep, then looks up. "Mark misses you."

I blink, surprised by the simplicity of what she just said. "Mark?"

"Yeah. And not just him. Everyone at the department does. You know how it is... we suck at saying it out loud. But it's true."

The statement lands somewhere between guilt and disbelief, like she just told me a stranger missed me. I swallow, searching for a response, but none comes.

After a minute, she shifts, crossing one leg over the other. The chair creaks under her. "Adams wanted me to give you a message."

I lean forward, brow lifting. "Is that so? Dare I ask what?"

Her eyes flick to the window, where rain trails down the glass in silver rivulets. She meets my gaze again. "She said it's time you knew now."

Something prickles down the back of my neck. I force a wry smile. "Let me guess, she arranged for her and me to get married?"

Both Darcy and Cassidy laugh.

"I'm pretty sure that happened months ago," Cassidy teases, and Anderson shakes her head, half-smiling.

Darcy shakes her head. "I think she is actually getting serious with this guy of hers. She is calming down a lot."

Cassidy bobs her head, and I feel a faint relief at the normalcy of it. I never thought those words would slip out of

Anderson without a laugh attached. She really has something big to tell me. I can feel it.

Then Anderson leans forward. “She wanted you to know that work is really boring without you.”

I laugh a spurt of relief. "You had me thinking it was something serious."

Darcy chuckles.

Cassidy shifts the conversation to the huge elephant in the room. “How’s Merrick doing?”

Anderson lets out a slow breath. Her eyes soften. “Surprisingly well. All things considered. He’s been keeping busy with work. Quiet. Healing, I think.”

I nod, but the walls close in. My chest constricts; a hot, wired pressure crawls up my throat, and settles behind my eyes.

I need a moment to myself.

“I’m gonna hit the bathroom,” I announce.

Cassidy looks up at me, worried again, but doesn’t say anything. I walk down the hall, close the bathroom door behind me, and brace my hands on the sink. My reflection is a scary sight. Dark circles under my eyes. It looks like I haven't slept in days. I grip the vanity with extreme force, and for a second, I wonder if cracking the sink would feel better than cracking myself open.

I soak a washcloth in cold water and lay it on my face for a moment. I won't lie; if it had suffocated me in that moment, I probably wouldn't have fought it. The thought flashes by quickly, and I shove it down before it takes root.

I can't talk about Merrick. Not yet. Not in front of anyone.

When I return, Anderson's waiting with that cop-look I hate. The one that means *this part's going to screw you good.* Her lips are pressed flat, the way they get when she hates what she's about to say.

She meets my gaze and tilts her head. "Karrie Cunningham reached out again. She really wants to talk to you."

A dry edge creeps into my voice. "Did she say which case this is about?" I lift my glass and take a long swallow.

Anderson's nod comes slow, relentless. Her eyes darken with seriousness. "The Bevin Stanley case."

My throat constricts. I cough, half-choke, and spray liquid across Cassidy's folded blanket. The wet spots spread like ink seeping through paper.

"You're fucking serious?" My voice sounds strangled.

"Dead serious," Anderson replies. She pauses, then her words land like a hammer. "I wanted to give you time. I know you're not on active duty, but Caleb... she's only willing to speak with you. And this could be important. Really important."

I can feel my pulse banging in my neck.

The room goes still. Even the rain against the window hushes.

Bevin Stanley.

Sixteen years old. Vanished five years ago on a Tuesday morning.

That case has burrowed into my marrow like a winter chill that never leaves. We suspected the family... the father with his twitchy hands and yellowed teeth, the mother with mascara-stained cheeks and bruises she blamed on clumsiness. Trafficking their own daughter to pay off debts. But we could never prove a damn thing. No body in the woods. No evidence that would stand up in a courtroom. Just the acid burn of intuition in my gut that something putrid festered behind that peeling blue front door.

The girl with the chipped purple nail polish and those quiet hazel eyes that seemed to hold secrets like anchors. I still see her. In dreams where she's running down endless hallways. In crosswalks where teenage girls with similar honey-brown hair make my heart stop. In the faces of kids that look like her. Sometimes I catch myself scanning crowds for her without even realizing I'm doing it.

That case...

That case was probably one of the reasons Samantha and I never worked out. I couldn't let it go, and she couldn't watch me unravel over it anymore, coming home at 3AM with bloodshot eyes and case files spread across our kitchen table.

But now Karrie Cunningham wants to talk? And why after five years of deafening silence?

"Why now?" I blurt out.

Anderson shrugs, her silver earrings catching the light. "Maybe what happened with the Fletchers shook something loose. Sometimes one tragedy wakes another."

Cassidy reaches out, sets her hand on my knee. Grounding me. Just like she always does. Her touch sends a small, steady warmth through me, like the first sip of whiskey on a cold night.

Anderson stands, brushing imaginary lint from her pants. "I'll give you her number. But don't wait too long. If she's ready to talk, we need to listen."

She says goodbye and disappears out the door, leaving only her words behind. Words as heavy as the clouds outside.

Just maybe, one of the burdens in the Fletcher case is a blessing for Bevin Stanley's family. Maybe now, a girl who vanished into nothing but case files and faded missing posters might finally be found. Or at least, maybe her story will stop screaming in the dark where no one can hear it.

CHAPTER 4

CALEB

We'd settled on a tiny, tucked-away park off a Spokane side street, the kind of hidden refuge where towering pines and cottonwoods press so close you almost forget there's a road ten yards away. A cracked asphalt trail winds along the riverbank, its ragged edges smothered in emerald moss and damp, russet leaves. Rusted benches, their metal legs bowed and weary, sag under years of neglect, while half-bare branches overhead shiver in the breeze, scattering mottled sunlight on the ground. Only the two of us, which is exactly the isolation she'd asked for.

When I pull into the gravel lot, Karrie's already sitting on a picnic table like she's afraid the bench part might swallow her whole. Her hood's up even though it's not raining. The cotton sleeves droop past her knuckles, like she's trying to disappear into the fabric itself. There's a half-crushed energy drink beside her.

She doesn't stand when I approach... only lifts her chin in a small nod. Her cheeks are blotched pink, streaked where tears have trailed down to her jawline.

"Miss Cunningham," I say, stopping two feet away.

"Just call me Karrie," she barks back. Her voice cracks halfway through the sentence, and she clears her throat like she's trying to scrape the emotion from it.

We sit in silence for a moment. I wait for her to speak of Bevin. Instead, she stares at her forearms, twisting the cuff of her sleeve. Her foot taps the bench.

"I miss Corey," she finally blurts out.

I close my eyes and exhale.

Of course she does.

"I keep thinking..." She wipes at her nose. "Maybe if I'd said something sooner..." She swallows, the hood shifting on her head. "I don't know. I just wish I'd done more to save him."

I've learned to meet grief with calm, professional distance, but today my defenses feel brittle. Let's face it, I am weak as fuck.

I lean forward and rest a hand on her shoulder. "You cared about him, Karrie. That much is obvious."

She shakes her head, mascara tears carving thin black lines down her cheeks. A sob wells in her throat. "He was the only one who ever really saw me. Not what I pretended to be... just me."

There's a fierce tenderness in that confession, like a shaft of sunlight through weathered wood.

Anyone could see that she loved Corey. The kind of love that sticks around even after someone's gone.

Suddenly, a yell cracks the hush. Two slurring voices to our right. One man shoves the other against a rusty garbage can; beer bottles clink in the grass as they stagger. Their curses ricochet through the trees. Even the birds go silent at the ruckus. Karrie glances over, then back at me.

"Should we do something?" she whispers.

I shake my head. "That's not why we're here."

Her gaze drifts upward to a cluster of robins launching from a crooked branch above us. She follows their flight until they vanish into the bright sky. "I always loved watching birds," she murmurs. "No matter where they are, they always know which way to go."

I nod, letting the moment stretch. The wind tugs at my collar, cool against my skin, and I hear my own heartbeat.

At last she exhales and turns to me with steady resolve in

her eyes. "I know you think the family had something to do with Bevin Stanley's disappearance."

I arch an eyebrow. "No comment."

A faint, wry smile crosses her lips. "Such a cop answer."

I scoff. "And what do you know about the Bevin Stanley case?"

She reaches into her hoodie pocket and extracts a dog-eared photograph, edges curled from constant folding. She smooths it with trembling fingers and hands it to me. My pulse kicks up as I unfold it.

"She was last seen with her science teacher," she confesses.

In the image, Bevin Stanley is perched sideways on a man's lap. The thin straps of her floral sundress have slipped off one shoulder, revealing pale skin and the tension in her collarbone. The man's goatee is trimmed razor-sharp; his thick-rimmed glasses glint in the sun. He's pressing his lips to her cheek with an intimacy that dissolves any pretense of a platonic friendship.

Bevin looks no older than sixteen; his face could belong to a man in his thirties.

"This guy's got to be what... thirty?"

"His name's Nick Bower," Karrie answers, eyes fixed on the picnic table. "He was twenty-eight then."

"How do you know that?" I question.

She swallows so hard that I can hear the gulp. "I took the photo."

The wind dies down. Or maybe I just stop hearing it.

I stare at her, disbelief souring in my gut. "You what?"

Tears gather in her eyes. She presses her fists inside her sleeves. "I knew about them. Thought it was wrong, but Bevin told me she loved him. She said they were going to run away together."

My throat goes dry. "And you didn't report it?"

Her bottom lip quivers. "I didn't want to get him in trouble."

"Why the hell not?"

Her voice drops to a whisper, so soft I lean in to catch it. "He's my stepbrother."

Holy shit in a handbasket.

Shock slams into me like a freight train. Stepbrother. The lead I've chased for five years lands in my lap like a thunderbolt. The air feels suddenly colder, like the truth itself stole the heat from the day.

Bevin Stanley is no longer a ghost. Someone named Nick Bower might hold every answer.

I point the photo at her with my hand. "And you're telling

me now because...?" I force the words past the tightening in my chest.

She grins. "Because I know you won't charge me for hiding evidence," she warns me.

A bitter laugh escapes me. "And how do you figure that?"

Her smile widens. "Because I know what Detective Adams did. You two went undercover without permission, used evidence she shouldn't have had. Evidence I am pretty damn sure she obtained illegally. I don't think your chief would be thrilled to learn that, would he?"

Damn it!

She's fucking blackmailing me.

Under any other circumstances, I'd shut her down instantly. But I need this photo. I need Nick Bower.

I'm going to solve this case once and for all.

I close my eyes for a moment, letting the weight of it settle. Then I lift my gaze and ask the question that's haunted every sleepless night since Bevin vanished: "Is she still alive?" The words scrape out of me, thin and desperate.

Please say yes.

Karrie's shoulders tremble with sobs. I see the guilt etched on her face, revealing just how much she truly cared for Bevin. Her breath stutters like someone trying to outrun their own memories.

Her lip trembles, then catches between her teeth as she struggles to hold herself together. “I don’t know.”

CHAPTER 5

CALEB

I step out onto the wide, weathered steps in front of the school. Dawn's pale light casts long shadows across the cement. I trail my fingertips along the iron railing, its cold paint peeling under my touch, bracing myself for the call I'm about to make.

Detective Anderson picks up on the second ring. "Reed, what's up?"

"I've got something," I say, keeping my voice low. "I have to hurry. I'm about to go into that class."

"Go on," she says.

I tuck my chin against the wind. "Karrie Cunningham gave me a photo. Says the last person to see Bevin was her science teacher."

There's a pause so deep I can practically hear the static on her end. "You're fucking kidding me."

"Not at all."

On her end, I hear the click of a pen tapping against a desk, the faint scrape of paper. She's already shifting into detective mode. "What's the teacher's name?"

"Nick Bower. She says he was twenty-eight at the time. In the photo, Bevin's sitting on his lap, and he's kissing her cheek."

"Jesus. A man of his age with a sixteen-year-old." She makes a shiver sound of disgust.

"I need you to look into him. Quietly. No mentions in the department."

"Do you think Karrie's playing you?"

"She didn't strike me as lying," I cut in, rubbing my hand over my jaw. "But honestly, I've been off my game on intuition lately."

Anderson lets out a breath. "Alright. I'll start digging. School records, old HR logs, anything I can find. If he taught her, there'll be a trail."

"Thanks," I tell her.

"Anything else?"

"No, that's all."

"Well, then..." she adds dryly, "good luck with the seminar. Heard you're guest-starring as the traumatized cop in front of fifty caffeinated law students."

"Don't remind me."

She chuckles. "Try not to swear too much."

I hang up the phone before she can say more. Otherwise, we will continue the back and forth, and I will be late.

As I walk back into the school, my palms start sweating, and I regret saying yes to this. I'm not built for this public-speaking bullshit. Never have been.

People watching me. Waiting to be impressed. Waiting to be inspired. I'm not an inspiration.

Hell, I barely get through my days anymore.

I finish the last of my water, the bottle crumpling like brittle paper in my hand, and toss it into a metal bin. It clatters against paper cups and snack wrappers. The lecture hall door groans as I push it open, and every pair of eyes swivels toward me, as though I've just stepped onto a stage bathed in judgment.

I navigate the aisle of sloping seats, the carpeted steps muffling my footsteps. I step up to the podium, fingers grazing the cool metal of the microphone stand. I flip a small switch; the mic emits a piercing squeal that makes me flinch.

I clear my throat. "I'm Detective Caleb Reed," I say, voice steady despite the tremor I feel. "I was asked to speak with you today about my first high-profile case. This goes back to 2006."

Pens stop moving. Conversations die. A girl in the front row closes her laptop like she's afraid to miss a single word.

"It involved six teenagers. All of them disappeared the same day: Marcus Davis. Paco Garcia. Levi Tucker. Sofia Lopez. Keisha Jones. And Bethany Taylor."

I pause, letting each name settle like a stone in everyone's gut.

"They spent ten days where no human being should ever be. Ten days in a place darker than hell. And somehow... they all survived." I let that settle for a moment, then continue. "And sometimes... survival is the closest thing to justice you're gonna get."

I scan their faces. They need the truth.

This isn't Law & Order. It's fluorescent-lit interrogation rooms, bleach that can't erase what you've seen, and the nightmares you learn to live with. It's the rare lead that blindsides you... like a woman with a photo and a secret finally desperate to be told.

"Today, I want to take you through a case that tested every limit of our legal system and left its mark on my career. I'll walk you through the hell those kids endured, beginning on a summer morning much like this one...."

CHAPTER 6

DAY ONE

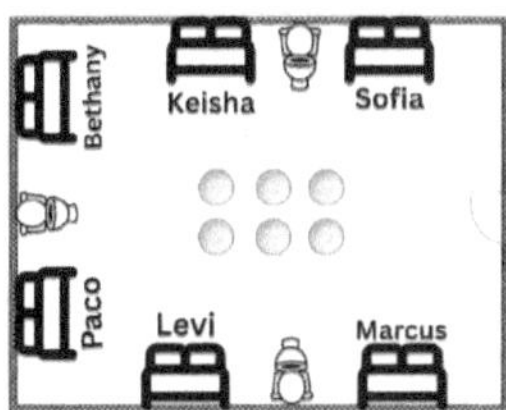

The low throbbing hum of distant engines was the only thing slicing through the suffocating blackness.

Paco blinked, his vision swarming with shadows.

Why can't I see?

The darkness pressed against his eyes, refusing to give anything back. He rubbed his eyes so hard his fingertips stung, as if he could scrape away the gloom and make sense of the nothingness. His heart pounded when the dark didn't change. His throat felt raw when he finally croaked, "Where am I? What is this place?"

A few feet away, Bethany lay on a narrow cot. Her breaths

came sharp and shallow, like she was drowning on air. She tried to speak, but all that came was a trembling whisper: "I don't know. What's happening?" Panic caught her throat, each word a ragged gasp. Her mind raced ahead of her body, jumping to worst-case answers she didn't want to name.

A sudden jangle of chains broke her question like glass. Keisha bolted upright, metal links rattling against her ankle cuff. The cold steel bit into her skin. She clawed at it instinctively. "What's going on? Why am I chained up?" she screamed, desperation bleeding through every syllable.

Levi's guttural roar echoed off the cement walls. "It's pitch black!" He thrashed his leg against its restraint, sparks of pain shooting up his calf. "What the hell is happening?"

If I don't sound calm, they'll panic more. "I don't know who you all are, but we gotta get out of here," Marcus growled beside him, the chain's clink a mocking chorus. His voice was steady, but his breathing wasn't.

Groggy and bleary, Sofia slumped against the cold concrete wall. "No shit," she mumbled, her words sluggish. "I feel like I've been drugged." A single droplet of water fell from somewhere overhead, plinking against her forehead. She flinched, shrieking, "What the fuck was that?"

Levi groaned, clutching his head as he pushed himself upright.

What did they do to us?

Every beat felt like a nail being hammered inside Levi's skull. "How did we end up here?" he asked, a mixture of fear and anger in his voice. He scanned the darkness, but it only deepened the dread crawling through his chest. "Fuck. My head hurts bad."

None of them could remember how they'd come to this rotten cell—no clues, only an empty ache where memories should be.

"We need to stay calm," Marcus uttered, even though he didn't feel it. He felt like fear was crawling under his skin, looking for a way out. "There has to be a way outta here."

Keisha's eyes darted along the rough stone walls. *What if no one knows we're here?*

"Where do we even start?" Keisha asked.

Marcus lashed out, kicking his chain. The metal links groaned but held firm. The sound echoed back at them hopelessly. "We start by breaking these damn chains."

Keisha's gaze flitted upward, catching a sliver of pale light leaking through a barred window high on the opposite wall. The faint glow danced on the cement floor. Light meant outside. Outside meant people.

"Look," she hissed, pointing. "There's a window. Maybe we can signal someone."

Please let someone be out there, she pleaded in her mind.

Sofia pressed her palm to her forehead, her teeth clenching against the throbbing pain. Her thoughts kept slipping away before she could grab them. "I have a nasty headache... I can't think straight," she muttered, each word a struggle breaking free.

Levi's brow furrowed as he racked his memory. "I remember something..." He swallowed hard. Fear coiled tighter when the memory refused to surface. "I was on a date with a girl. And then..." His eyes went distant, haunted. "Nothing. I... I woke up here." His confession fell into the hush, offering no comfort.

Bethany's breaths shot out faster and faster as she hyperventilated. The walls were closing in on her, or at least that's what her mind insisted, pressing against her lungs.

Paco, hearing the tremble in her breath, inched closer. If he focused on helping her, maybe he wouldn't fall apart himself. "Look at me," he said, his eyes locking onto hers. "Give me your hand."

For a long, agonizing moment, she calculated whether to trust him... whether anyone could be trusted.

Paco's hand remained outstretched. "It's okay," he whispered. "I've got you."

With a tremor she couldn't quite hide, Bethany reached out, slipping her hand into his, like she was holding onto her last shred of hope. The cell's darkness felt alive, lifting. Something in Paco's tone reached into her terror, calming her breathing.

Beads of sweat traced lines through the dust on Keisha's forehead. Her voice cracked as she hurled her plea into the universe. "Help! Someone help us!" The sound ripped out of her, raw and unanswered. Each word torn from her throat.

Sofia's sobs rose in a raw, guttural chorus. Her body shuddered with every choked gasp, her arms clutching herself as though she could squeeze courage into her bones. "Why is this happening?" she wailed. "Please, anyone... help!"

Marcus's skull felt like it was splitting in two. The noise drilled straight into his head. With a thunderous roar, he clutched his temples and bellowed, "Shut the hell up!" Suddenly there was nothing but a brittle, ringing silence. Even the drip of a leaky pipe seemed to pause. Everyone turned to face him.

"I'm sorry," Marcus muttered, his voice softening as he rubbed his forehead. "But freaking out isn't going to help. It's making my headache worse." He took a deep breath, letting the tension slip from his shoulders as his eyes scanned the dim room. Marcus had always been the one to keep his cool under pressure, the guy with street smarts who could talk his way out of almost anything. If there were a way out of this pit, he would find it.

"Alright," he said. "Let's take stock of what we have. Any tools, anything at all that might help us break free?"

Paco raked a hand through his hair. "All I see are beds, toilets, and a barred window. How's any of that gonna help? Feels like we're trapped in a fucking Saw movie."

A fresh wave of panic surged through Keisha. Her legs threatened to give way. "Oh my God... we're all going to die!"

"Shhh!" Marcus shot her a hard look. "The hell we are," he snapped, but not unkindly. Determination cut through the fear in his voice. "Everyone, make yourselves useful and look around your space. We have to find something... *anything.*"

CHAPTER 7

DAY ONE

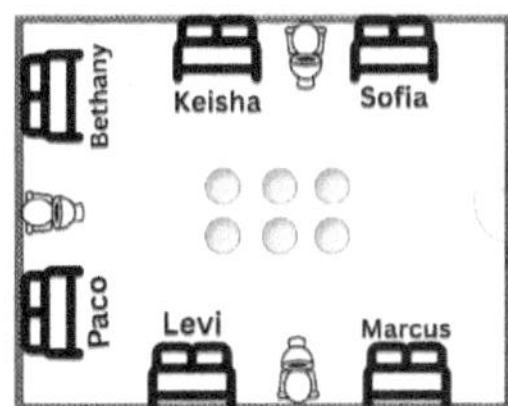

They began to study their surroundings more closely, eyes scanning every inch. Marcus examined his space, his fingers trailing along the gritty, cold floor. The rusted links of his chains clinked as he shifted. Every sound felt amplified, dangerous. His eyes scanned the area around his bed, taking in the grim scene... the toilet in the corner was a foul, grimy mess that made his nose wrinkle and stomach churn.

The stench hit him like a punch. "Gross! It smells so bad in here," he groaned under his breath, gagging slightly.

On the walls, he spotted faded graffiti, messages from previous captives, perhaps. His stomach tightened at the thought... people had been here before them. Most of the writing was indecipherable, jagged scratches and incoherent ramblings, but one phrase stood out: *Find the key.*

Paco, determined to be useful, scanned his area with renewed focus. His eyes fell on a loose brick near the base of the wall, its edges worn and cracked. His fingers twitched, and he crouched down, attempting to work the brick free.

Levi, growing more frustrated by the second, inspected his corner with a scowl. Anger was easier than fear. His bed looked identical to the others. But as his hand grazed the concrete, he noticed something different. A crack. Small but distinct, running jagged near his toilet.

Across the room, Keisha's legs felt like jelly. Her muscles trembled uncontrollably with each step she took. Her eyes drifted to her surroundings, but the sight of her stained, uninviting toilet only deepened the pit in her stomach. She swallowed hard, fighting the urge to gag. She stared at the words etched into her wall: *Nothing is what it seems.* The letters trembled before her, more chilling than the ice-cold floor beneath her feet.

Sofia's chest had tightened as her eyes flitted nervously from one shadowed corner of the cell to another. Her breath felt trapped, like it couldn't fully expand. Beside her, a stained metal toilet sat permanent as a tombstone, its cracked porcelain a constant mockery of their captivity. The walls, scarred by ragged claw marks and smeared with dark streaks that might have been blood or mold, twisted her stomach into knots.

Fuck me! We are going to die, Sofia thought, a scream trapped inside her.

Paco and Bethany shared a worried glance as their shackled ankles rattled against the cold iron of their beds. The thin chains bit into their skin each time they shifted, dragging their spirits deeper into despair. Their eyes drifted upward, landing on the single barred window high in the wall.

Paco's voice cut through the oppressive silence, fueled by hope. "Check out the window," he rasped. "Maybe there's a way..." His words died when something else snagged his attention: jagged letters carved deep into the cinderblock. He leaned forward, heart hammering, and read aloud, *"The key to freedom lies within all of you."*

In the opposite corner, Keisha's head snapped up at Paco's tone. Her skin prickled with dread. Her eyes widened as they locked onto her own message scrawled across the wall. "Mine says, 'Nothing is what it seems.'" She whispered it, each word hanging in the air like a dare. Or a warning.

Sofia let out a hollow laugh, perching on the edge of her bed. “Pretty sure it’s exactly what it seems. Or I’d be at home right now.”

A groan of discomfort broke the tension. “All I know is I have to use the bathroom really bad,” Marcus admitted, nodding toward the grimy toilet beside him. His face twisted with disgust.

Keisha winced, pressing a hand to her hip. “Me too,” she echoed, her urgency matching his.

Marcus rubbed the back of his neck. “Okay... we’ll take turns. The rest of us face the wall for a bit of privacy.” Even as he said it, the plan felt pathetic, but necessary.

Paco snorted. “You are joking, right?”

Marcus let out a dramatic sigh. “Do you see any other options, man? It’s the only way that gives us some privacy.” He wasn’t entirely convinced himself, but there weren’t many choices. None of them felt human anymore.

Reluctantly, they agreed. One by one, they shuffled forward. Marcus went first; the flush reverberated against the walls. Keisha followed, her face expressing embarrassment and disgust. Levi stood rigid against the wall, every muscle trembling to hide his shame.

Bethany hesitated before approaching the toilet. Her cheeks

burned as she avoided everyone's gaze. With a deep breath, she braced herself and quickly did her business, muttering under her breath, "This is so gross."

Sofia nodded, sitting on the edge of her bed with a grim expression. "You're telling me," she agreed.

Despite the awkwardness, a strained silence fell over the group as they forced themselves to look away and give each other what little dignity they could muster in this nightmare. As the group finished their turns at the toilet, they all sat on their beds.

Discomfort of hunger gnawed at their stomachs. Paco, shifting uncomfortably, finally voiced what they were all thinking. "I'm starving."

Keisha shot Marcus a pointed look. "Any ideas, boss?" Her tone dripped sarcasm, but worry lurked beneath.

Marcus gave her a dirty look. "Really? You wanna start..."

Before he could finish, Keisha cut him off. "Well, you seem to think you're the only one with a brain here."

Marcus let out a deep, growly sigh. "I'm just tryin' to make it through this like the rest of you."

Bethany interjected, attempting to diffuse the tension. "We can start by introducing ourselves. That way we have names to our faces."

Sofia nodded eagerly. “Good idea.”

The group fell silent for a moment, exchanging hesitant glances. Despite their dire situation, the act of sharing their names felt intimate, a strange vulnerability in a place that had stripped them of everything else. It made them real again.

Marcus cleared his throat. “I’m Marcus Davis. New Yorker here,” he said.

Keisha gasped, her eyes widening as the realization hit. “We’re not even from the same state,” she declared, glancing at each of them with growing unease. Hesitantly, she continued, “I’m Keisha Jones, from Nevada.”

Levi took a deep breath, hesitating for a moment before speaking up. “I’m Levi Tucker. I live in Colorado.”

Sofia, attempting a small smile despite the tension, introduced herself next. “My name is Sofia Lopez. I’m from Florida.”

“I’m Paco Garcia, from British Columbia. Am I the only one from Canada here?”

Bethany exhaled wearily. “I’m Bethany Taylor... also from Colorado.”

Marcus grunted. “The question is... where *are* we, and how did we all end up in this shithole?”

The responses died in everyone’s mouths as static crackled

overhead. Every head snapped up at once. A hidden speaker hummed to life. The voice that emerged was cold, with no hint of empathy: "First step is complete. Now, lie on your beds and prepare for the next step."

Marcus leapt to his feet, his fists clenched so tight his knuckles blanched. "Listen here, whoever the fuck you are..."

The voice sliced through his words like a scalpel. "Do not defy me. If you want out of here, you will do as I say. Now lie down on your bed and prepare for the next step."

The finality in the speaker's voice left little room for argument. Marcus retreated to his bed, the springs creaking beneath his weight.

Then, the creepy voice delivered its final chilling message. "Nighty night," he crooned, the false sweetness curdling in their ears.

A hissing sound erupted from above. Fine mist poured from ceiling vents, filling the room with a sickly-sweet fog that clung to their skin, invading their nostrils. The acrid taste coated their tongues as their eyelids grew heavy.

Marcus fought against it, his body trembling as he struggled to stay awake. His vision blurred, the corners of the room becoming nothing more than smudged shapes in the haze. "Stay... together..." he mumbled, his words slurring as his consciousness slipped away.

Keisha's heart pounded in her chest as she felt the fog envelop her. "No... not again..." she whispered, terror cracking her voice.

Levi's head spun, the edges of his vision darkening. He reached out, trying to grasp at anything to keep him grounded, but his strength waned.

Sofia's thoughts raced as the chemical filled her lungs. She tried to move, to scream, but her body felt like lead. "Help..." she tried to call out, but the word barely left her lips before her eyes fluttered shut against her will.

And then everything went dark.

CHAPTER 8

DAY TWO

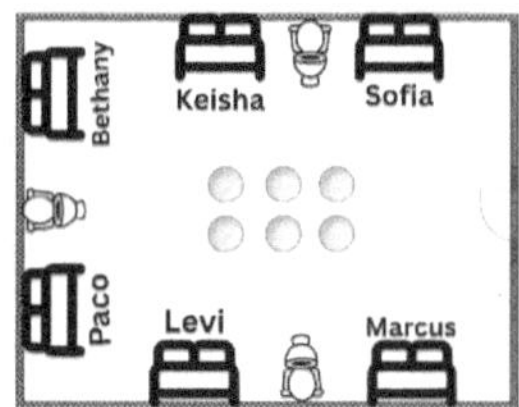

They stirred sluggishly, dragging themselves from the numb haze of forced sleep as pale shafts of morning light pried through the narrow, barred window overhead. In the center of the bare concrete floor sat six plates piled high with steaming food, an unexpected feast in this prison.

Paco's stomach roared so fiercely it eclipsed every instinct of caution. The sound embarrassed him, but hunger drowned out shame. He snapped upright and lunged forward. "I need to eat something," he growled, snatching a plate and nearly scalding his fingers on the hot rim. The burn barely registered compared to the ache in his gut.

Keisha hovered beside him, her eyes bright as she claimed her own dish. Steam curled toward her face, carrying the rich aroma of spices and roasted meat. She inhaled deeply, closing her eyes for just a second, as if it could chase away the horror of her situation.

Marcus lingered in the murky corner, creasing his brows. "Wait, what if..."

Sofia blurted out before Marcus could finish, "What if it is poisoned?" The word landed heavily, sucking the warmth from the room.

Levi blinked, confusion twisting his features in the half-light. "If they meant to poison us, do you think we'd even wake up after whatever the hell they smothered us with last night?" His voice shook despite the logic.

Paco nodded, biting into a savory chunk of meat. Juice splattered against his chin. The flavor hit him so hard he almost groaned. "Good enough for me. Dying of poison beats dying of starvation."

Keisha gave him a wry smile, wiping crumbs from her lips. "Good point."

Marcus shrugged, lowering his head to his plate. Suspicion warred with hunger, and hunger won. "Yeah, fuck it. Smells too good to pass up."

No one spoke as forks scraped against ceramic. Each began diving into the meal, savoring every bite. It was the first normal thing they'd done.

All except Bethany.

She remained seated on her bed, a single tear tracing a cold path down her cheek.

Why is this happening to us? I want to go home. The thought echoed, hollow and useless.

She watched the others eat. Her stomach knotted with hunger, but she forced herself to wait, her eyes darting around the room for any sign of danger. Any twitch. Any collapse. Any sign this was a trick. Fifteen agonizing minutes passed. Their faces remained healthy-looking, their breathing steady. No convulsions.

Paco glanced over, rubbing his belly. Relief softened his features. "Hey Chica, if you're not eating yours, can I?" he asked, eyeing her plate.

Bethany lifted her head, surprise flashing in her eyes. "I'm eating it," she snapped. "I just needed a moment." She picked up her fork and tore into the meal. The first bite nearly made her cry.

With the last crumb gone, the group leaned back against the stone walls, sighing in relief. Their bellies were full; their minds, momentarily clearer.

Sofia rubbed her temples. "We need a plan to get out of here. The last thing I remember is that voice saying the first step was completed."

Keisha's fingers drummed on her knee. Nervous energy crackled beneath her skin. "What the hell did that mean?"

Levi shook his head, eyes darting around the cell. "No fucking clue."

Marcus's face lit up with sudden realization. "It was right after we introduced ourselves to each other."

Before anyone could digest his words, a sharp click echoed through the room, followed by the crackle of the hidden speaker. The teens froze, every breath caught in their throats as the distorted, threatening voice dripped from the small grille overhead.

"Time for the first test. Your life depends on the actions of others. Your freedom rests on each of you. The player chosen for this round must answer correctly. If they fail... your captivity will stretch another day. Your fate hinges on how well this person has paid attention. Will step two begin today or tomorrow... that choice belongs to the impatient person who ate his food first."

Every pair of eyes swung to Paco. He stood by the cold

metal bunk with his shoulders hunched. His heart pounded so loudly he was certain they could all hear it.

Marcus's face, half-lit by the harsh light, was unreadable until a dangerous glint sparked in his eyes. "No pressure, dude... but you fucking better have paid attention," he snarled.

Frustration and fear boiled up in the cramped space like steam in a pressure cooker. The room felt too small for all of it. Paco clutched his hair, sinking onto his cot. His thoughts scrambled, rewinding through every moment.

"Great, so now we're all at the mercy of a split-second decision?" Sofia groaned, slamming her palm against the wall.

Keisha threw up her hands, glaring at the ceiling. "Why are we turning on each other? This isn't going to solve anything!"

Levi's voice rose above the others, edged with panic. "What if he gets it wrong? What then? We're just stuck here because of this guy."

Before Levi could go further, Keisha stepped forward, planting her feet on the cracked cement floor. "Enough! Blaming Paco won't change a damn thing."

Paco felt the weight of every accusing glare like a physical blow. It felt like hands pressing him down, crushing his ribs inward. His chest tightened, each breath hotter than the last, as the fear of failure hovered overhead like a dark cloud.

Amid the mounting chaos, Bethany's calm voice rang out, startling them all into silence. She met Paco's frantic eyes. "Threats won't help us. More fear will only cloud our minds." She nodded toward the darkened ceiling speaker. "If he fails, it isn't his fault... it's theirs."

Her words sank in like cool water on hot coals. They realized their anger was misplaced. The true enemy sat unseen, flicking switches in the shadows.

A click echoed from the ceiling. Cold, mocking laughter rattled the metal walls. "Ready or not, you better not have forgot."

Paco stood up, steeling himself for what was to come. "Let's get this over with." Then he looked up at the speaker. "What is it?" he shouted.

"Don't you raise your voice to me," the speaker hissed, each word weighted with menace. It inhaled three slow, echoing breaths... like a predator weighing its prey. "What is the person's name to your right?"

Paco's mind spun helplessly as he locked onto Levi's startled face.

Shit! What the hell was his name?

His thoughts scattered, slippery and useless. He glanced to

his left.

That is Bethany.

He looked at Marcus, who was giving him the look of death.

That's MARC-ASS.

Even now, his brain clung to stupid humor to survive.

He turned his attention to the other two girls, both extremely attractive to Paco, offering a brief distraction.

Her name is Keisha.

The other girl's name... he couldn't remember. He just calls her his dream woman in his mind.

He looked back at Levi, his mind racing for an answer.

We are so fucked. Think man!

He recalled the moment Levi had introduced himself.

I'm... I'm from Colorado. I'm Lee, from Colorado. Ugh! Doesn't sound right.

It sounded wrong, half-remembered.

Above him, the speaker taunted softly: "I have all the time in the world."

Marcus's voice boomed in reply, raw and desperate. "Well... we don't!"

Paco's eyes roamed over Marcus's rumpled jeans. A name emerged from the depths of his mind.

Levi!

That has to be it.

He wasn't one-hundred percent certain, but it resonated louder than "Lee." It felt right.

He drew in a ragged breath, his palm slick against his scalp. The damp stench of concrete pressed in on him as he met Marcus's expectant stare. "His name is..." His voice caught like a lurching train. He swallowed, lifted his chin. "Levi," he croaked.

"Is that your final answer?" The speaker's tinny voice cut through the silence.

Shit! Did that sound like I have it wrong? "No." Levi looked at Paco with relief in his eyes. "I mean, yes. That is my final answer. Levi!"

A distorted chuckle crackled overhead. "Your answer is wrong. That is not their name."

A collective exhale shivered through the group, bodies slumping as though the air had thickened. Fear slammed back into them all at once.

CHAPTER 9

DAY TWO

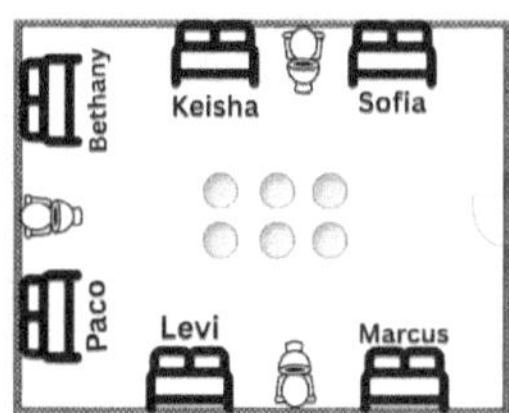

Sofia's voice rumbled. "Yes... it is. I remember all of their names."

The speaker interjected, cold and clinical. "Let me finish. You are wrong... that is not his name. However, you passed the test because that is the name that was introduced."

Levi's eyes widened. Confusion rippled through the others... relief warred with betrayal. Something ugly lurked beneath the relief.

Marcus's jaw clenched. "What the hell, man? Why are you lying to us?"

Levi's shoulders curled inward. "I'm not lying. My name

is Levi." His voice trembled as memories surged, a PTSD flashback from childhood embarrassment and pain.

Keisha's voice pierced the tension. "What the hell is happening? Someone's lying."

Bethany's tone dripped with impatience. "Can we just focus on step two? We passed. Who cares what that guy's real name is? Let's move on and get out of here."

Paco's throat tightened. Even though he'd passed the test, adrenaline clawed at his veins. Victory felt hollow. He couldn't shake the fear that he'd ruined everything.

Levi remained silent, refusing to meet anyone's gaze. He wouldn't take his eyes off the floor. I'm not ready to have this conversation, he thought to himself.

"Bethany's right," Sofia muttered, voice low but steel-edged. "We need to focus on step two."

Marcus glared at the speaker panel. "We're waiting... what is step two, jackass?"

"I will not ask for respect again. Step two starts tomorrow." The group groaned. "Blame your mouthy friend here. Like I said... your freedom depends on each other." The line went dead.

A low hum of discontent coursed through the cell. Paco's anger snapped. He whirled on Marcus. "This is your fault!

Quit talking back to the psycho that has us in here. How stupid are you?"

Marcus's usual spark was extinguished. His shoulders sagged; his head dropped. Not a single armed retort came. For the first time since they'd been sealed in this damp tomb, Marcus was speechless... aware he'd screwed them all.

In the corner, Levi sat rigid, as though the walls themselves had caged him. His gaze drifted past the scene, sinking into the twilight of a memory he'd fought to forget. He reflected on a pivotal moment in his life. The one when he told his parents about his true self.

The cell dissolved around him.

Levi sat at the kitchen table, his heart pounding in his chest as he mustered the courage to speak his truth. His hands clasped tightly together, fingers trembling with nervous anticipation. His parents sat across from him, their expressions a mix of curiosity and apprehension.

"Mom, Dad... there's something important I need to tell you. It's about who I really am. I'm not your daughter; I've never felt like one. I'm your son. And... I want you to call me Levi."

His words hung in the air, the weight of his revelation heavy in the room. This was the bravest moment of his life. His mother's face softened, a mixture of surprise and understanding dawning in her eyes. But his father's reaction was different, his features contorted with disbelief and then anger.

"It took courage to say that," his mother had said gently. "I love you, no matter what."

His father had laughed... a bitter, hollow sound. The kind that cuts deep. "Levi? Don't be ridiculous. You're Amber. You were born a girl, and that's that. This is just a dumb phase."

Levi had clenched his fists. "It's not a phase, Dad. I've felt wrong in my body for as long as I can remember."

"Yes! You are. I've changed your diapers. End of discussion," his father snapped, his voice filled with frustration and denial.

"Please let's try to understand and support her. It's going to take time for all of us to adjust, but she's still our child," Levi's mom pleaded, tears welling up in her eyes.

"He... Mom, stop saying she," Levi had choked out, his voice raw with hurt.

Levi's mother collapsed into sobs, her shoulders heaving as if they bore the world's weight. Tears streamed down her cheeks, each one a spark of grief. His father's face had gone the color of burning embers as he bellowed, "How dare you upset your mother like that!" His voice cracked with rage. "Get to your room now. Grow the hell up."

Levi's heart thudded against his ribcage like a war drum, each beat echoing the tumultuous battle raging within him. His eyes flickered with vulnerability as a solitary tear escaped, tracing a path down his cheek, a silent testament to the inner turmoil consuming him. He stole a quick glance at the group.

I just wanted one moment in my life where I could be who I really am. No questions, no judgments.

Reality crashed down upon him like a tidal wave.

How does this lunatic know my other name?

Levi's pulse quickened, his skin prickling with unease. He inhaled, the stale air filling his lungs, and forced the words out.

"Hey, guys," he began, voice trembling so much it sounded foreign to him. "I need to tell you something. My name is Levi, but I was born with another name." His chest heaved. "I'm transsexual."

In the sudden hush, Keisha's eyes widened until they nearly swallowed her face; a flicker of understanding sparkled in her gaze.

Paco and Sofia exchanged a brief look. "What's that mean?"

Paco asked.

Keisha blurted out, "It means someone was born in the wrong body."

Bethany looked surprised. "How? What do you mean?"

Keisha sighed. "I don't know how to explain it."

Levi spoke up. "My therapist said that it means I'm a male born in a female body."

Paco and Bethany stared at him. Not with judgement, but with surprise that something like that could actually happen.

Even Marcus, who usually snapped out barbed quips, lifted his chin and nodded, his usual smirk replaced by something softer, deeper.

Levi's throat constricted. Every fiber of his being begged him to flee, but he pressed on. "I really hope this doesn't change how you see me."

Paco's hand shot out, his grip warm and steady on Levi's wrist. "We've got your back," he said, voice low and firm.

Sofia nodded in agreement. "You are part of this group, no matter what."

Even Marcus cleared his throat, his eyes shining with uncharacteristic sincerity. "You'll always be Levi to us. That crazy lunatic can fuck right off with his games."

A surge of relief and gratitude welled up inside Levi, and

he blinked back tears. In that cramped, buzzing room, surrounded by flickering lights, he finally felt seen... accepted. The ache of his family's rejection still throbbed, but here, among strangers, it felt a little less brutal. He managed a shaky smile and whispered, "Thanks."

Another click resonated from the ceiling. "Step two completed," the disembodied voice announced. "You have ten minutes to wrap up. Then, you need to lie down, and prepare for step three."

Panic rippled through the group like electricity. In a silent agreement, they took turns doing their business. After they all used the toilets and returned to their beds, a heavy silence settled over the room.

They knew what was coming.

Then the mist appeared. It seeped from vents, curling around them like a living thing.

CHAPTER 10

DAY THREE

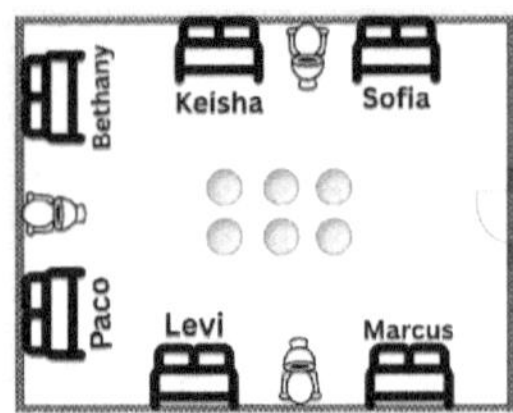

They woke to the same nightmare. Consciousness crept back slowly, heavy and wrong. As eyelids peeled open, they spotted food plates arranged on the floor again. Only this time the plates held fresh fruit slices, neatly made sandwiches, and bottles of water.

Hunger ripped through them. They didn't hesitate. Their aching stomachs drove them forward, and within seconds they'd each snatched a plate. The room filled with the wet smack of chewing, like a pack of famished dogs tearing at a carcass.

Sofia's hand paused mid-reach for a turkey sandwich. Her

throat tightened. A single, glossy photograph lay on the stained concrete beside her plate, and its edges were smudged; it was an obituary portrait. Her pulse hammered in her ears as she recognized the face. Pale newborn features staring back at her. Her twin brother, Anthony, who'd died at birth. A face she'd only seen in pictures. A life that never had a chance.

Her plate clattered to the floor. Tears stung her eyes as she clutched the photograph. The world narrowed to that image. A choked sob ripped from her throat. "What kind of sick joke is this?" she screamed into the bare walls, voice echoing toward the hidden speaker she knew was watching.

The others stopped eating and stared at her. Hunger drained from their faces, replaced by unease. Confusion was etched on every face. Keisha slid forward, concern flickering in her eyes. She moved slowly, like she might startle Sofia if she rushed. "Sofia, what's wrong?"

Holding the photo as if it might burn her, Sofia's tears spilled down her cheeks. Her hands shook violently. "This..." her voice cracked, "this is my twin." She shook the picture. "He died at birth. Why does this... this psycho have this?"

Keisha's expression softened. Her anger gave way to empathy. "I'm so sorry."

Marcus's face burned with anger. He knelt beside her and

shouted at the ceiling vent, "Is this some kind of twisted game to you?" His voice quivered with fury.

Silence mocked them.

Sofia thought back to a conversation she had with her mother not too long ago. The memory surfaced uninvited, dragging her away from the cell and into the past.

"Mom," she began, her voice hesitant, hands twisting nervously in her lap, "can we talk about Anthony?"

Her mother looked up from the newspaper, her eyes reflecting a mixture of sorrow and understanding. The paper lowered slowly, as if she already knew where this was going. She nodded gently, inviting Sofia to share her thoughts.

Sofia took another deep breath. Her chest felt tight, like she was opening a door she'd kept locked for years. "I've always wondered about him. What it would have been like to have my twin brother growing up. I've imagined us playing together, sharing secrets, and facing the world side by side."

Her mother's eyes softened, and she reached across the table to place a comforting hand on Sofia's. "Sweetheart, I know it's not easy. Losing Anthony was one of the hardest moments of our lives."

Sofia nodded, her throat tightening with emotions she had long kept buried. "I've always wanted to ask... what happened in the delivery room?"

Her mother took a moment to collect her thoughts before speaking. Her gaze drifted somewhere far away, back in time. "The delivery was difficult, Sofia. You and Anthony were born prematurely, and the medical team did everything they could to save both of you. But Anthony was very fragile, and despite their efforts, he didn't make it."

Sofia felt a lump forming in her throat, tears welling up in her eyes. The image of a delicate baby brother she had never known flashed through her mind.

"Did you get to see him right away?" Sofia asked, her voice cracking.

"No. They took you both out of the room. You each had a medical team working on you to get you stable. I was able to see you first. It didn't take long to know something was wrong with your brother."

"Did you get to see him while he was..." Sofia paused. The word lodged in her throat, refusing to come out, but her mom knew what she meant.

"No, he passed before we got the chance to see him. I can't explain the feeling of seeing my son lifeless. It was the most horrendous pain I ever experienced." Sofia's mother hid her face, trying to hide the tears. "Sorry, I can't talk about this

anymore." Her mother squeezed Sofia's hand. "We will never forget Anthony. He'll always be a part of our family, even if he's not physically here. And I know he watches over you, proud of the incredible person you've become."

The memory shattered, dissolving back into the cold concrete cell.

Marcus's voice cut through the lingering ache. "He's trying to break us," he told them. "We need to stay focused. Don't let him get to you."

Sofia passed the photo around, and the others examined it with solemn faces. When it reached Paco, he looked at the image with a pained expression.

"I'm sorry for your loss," Paco muttered. "Losing a twin must be hard. I grew up with no siblings. Always wanted one. I can't imagine what you went through."

Sofia nodded, appreciating his words but still consumed by grief. "It's... it's a different loss," she muttered. "I never got to know him, but it's like a part of me has always been missing."

Paco hesitated, then confessed, his jaw tightening as he swallowed memories he'd rather forget. "I lost my mother a few years ago. It's been hard."

A hush fell. Each of them stared at the meager feast... once so inviting, now a cruel reminder of their captor's power.

"We need to stay strong," Marcus stated, breaking the silence. "Whatever game this person is playing, we can't let them win."

They nodded, though the tremor in their bodies betrayed their fear. They picked at the food again, each bite heavy with anxiety.

Bethany watched Paco, hesitation flickering in her gaze. She swallowed a bite of melon, then asked quietly, "How did your mom die, Paco?"

Paco closed his eyes, recalling that day. "She got hit by a drunk driver. He's rotting in jail now." His eyes flicked to the ceiling, as though the speaker might judge him for speaking.

A tear slid down Bethany's cheek. She blinked quickly, trying to hide it. "I'm so sorry."

He met Bethany's sympathetic stare. "Life keeps going."

Levi sat apart from the group, lost in his own thoughts. He pictured Stefany's face, imagining her confusion and hurt when she never heard from him again.

She probably thinks I ghosted her. I'm going to lose her.

He shook his head, trying to dispel the despair creeping in. He glanced around at the others. "We need to get the hell out of here."

Marcus shot him a dark look. "No shit. That's what I've

been saying."

Sofia's grief burst into anger. She spat, "Oh, shut up already! This guy owns us now. All we can do is follow his orders." She stomped her foot, then hurled her brother's photo across the bed.

Keisha shouted at the ceiling, "What's step three, huh? You damn lunatic!"

A click sounded in the ceiling. The room went deathly quiet again. Then a smooth, mocking voice drifted down: "Call me Dynamo." It exhaled a sigh of impatience that felt like a slap against their ears.

The group exchanged uneasy glances. The voice, now named Dynamo, continued, its tone smooth and mocking. "You see, you're all part of a very special experiment. You'll play the roles I've assigned, whether you like it or not."

Sofia balled her fists and glared at the hidden vent. "What do you want from us?" she demanded.

A low, malevolent chuckle had rumbled from Dynamo. "What I want is for you to learn. To understand the truths about yourselves and each other. This is about growth, my dear. Painful, necessary growth."

Marcus sprang to his feet, pacing his small area of floor space, fighting to contain his fury. "You're sick," he snarled.

"We're not your playthings."

Dynamo sighed theatrically. "But you are, Marcus. This game is far larger than any of you. You'll thank me someday."

Levi's face twisted in disbelief. He hurled his voice at the speaker, veins standing out on his neck. "Thank... you? For what? For torturing us?"

Dynamo's tone dropped to icy calm. "For enlightening you. Now, step three will commence shortly. Be prepared."

Then the speaker clicked off, plunging the cramped room back into oppressive silence.

Keisha collapsed onto the bed, shoulders heaving, hair plastered to her forehead with sweat. "What are we going to do?" she'd whispered. "How do we prepare for something when we don't even know what it is?"

Bethany rubbed her palms together, eyes darting to the scuffed walls. "Maybe we are already doing step three. He did tell us to get to know each other."

Keisha glanced down at her shaking hands. "Since we got the photo of Sofia's brother today, maybe we're supposed to share losses today."

Marcus snorted, pacing again. "Who knows?"

Levi cleared his throat. "Has anyone else lost an immediate family member?"

Only Paco and Sofia whispered yes. The rest shook their heads to suggest otherwise.

Marcus stopped mid-stride and stared at the group. "So if only Paco and Sofia lost someone, that can't be what ties all of us together."

The group murmured in agreement, each lost in their own thoughts. The connection between Paco and Sofia was clear, but what linked the rest of them? Their captor's game was becoming twisted and complex.

Dynamo's voice crackled over the speaker. "Step three is complete. Time for test number two. Since Marcus fancies himself a genius, he'll answer the next question."

Marcus's jaw hardened as he glared upward. "What do you want from us now?"

"Simple, Marcus. Answer correctly, and you move on. Answer incorrectly, and you do not."

Marcus squared his shoulders, hiding the tremor in his chest. "Fine. What's the question?"

"Where is Keisha from?"

Marcus had thrown back his head and laughed, bitter and hollow. "Seriously? This is fucking ridiculous."

He'd watched the mixture of fear and hope in the other's eyes, then dove into memory searching for a link.

I'm pretty sure she was the one from my birth state, Marcus thought to himself. *Since he's looking for links, I'm going with that.*

With his heart pounding, Marcus crossed his sweaty fingers behind his back and declared, "Nevada."

A breath had held in the room. "You are correct."

A collective, ragged exhale had filled the space.

Keisha mumbled, "Thank God!"

Dynamo's voice snapped them back. "You know what time it is. You have ten minutes."

Click. The speaker died. For a heartbeat, they all just stared at one another, relief mingled with dread.

Marcus ran a hand across his sweaty forehead and met their eyes. "We did it. For now, at least."

Bethany stepped closer, awe and fear flickering in her gaze. "How did you figure it out?"

Marcus leaned back against the cold wall, exhaustion and a spark of pride in his voice. "It's all about links. And I was born in Nevada."

CHAPTER 11

DAY FOUR

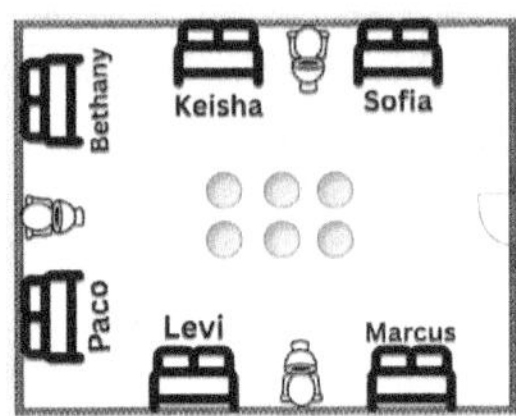

Keisha's eyelids fluttered open first, and the stale tang of grease and charred bacon drifted through the cramped chamber. Bacon and eggs are on the menu this morning.

One by one, the others surfaced from their uneasy slumber: Sofia pressed trembling fingertips to her temples, wiping away the last vestiges of sleep; Paco's low grunt rumbled against the concrete floor; Levi stretched so sharply his spine sounded like a broken twig; Bethany rose with a slow, exasperated sigh, shoulders sagging under some invisible weight.

Marcus was the last to rise.

They leaned forward over mismatched plastic plates like

starving animals, shoveling down a meager pile of bacon so overcooked it snapped with each bite, and eggs so underdone they slid across the plate like wet clay. To leave any of it uneaten was unthinkable under Dynamo's unpredictable rules.

Next to Marcus's plate sat a tiny, ridiculously cheerful blue party hat... its bright plastic rim mocking him in the harsh fluorescent glare.

He paused, fingers hovering over it. The rest of them noticed it too, but no one spoke.

Marcus swallowed hard, mind drifting back to the night he was taken. His eighteenth birthday.

He'd been sitting across from his girlfriend in their favorite downtown restaurant... her hair pulled back, her laugh bubbling up at everything he said. They ordered cheesecake with one candle, and he'd leaned over the table, feeling bold, feeling in love, and said, *"One day I'm gonna marry you, you know."*

She'd laughed, like she always did when he got sentimental. Laughed it off. Teased him about being dramatic.

Now he wondered if she thought he'd left her. Got bored with her.

Does she think I'm avoiding her? Has she found someone else?

The idea of her with another guy made him queasy.

He stared at the plastic hat. In a voice so soft it barely rose above the clatter of cutlery, he breathed, "I miss you, baby."

All around him, the others jabbered over bacon counts and egg yolk jokes, but he was a world away.

Finally, Paco pointed at the hat with his plastic fork. "So... I'm just gonna say it. The clue of the day is clearly the birthday hat."

Marcus didn't even look up. "Probably because it was my birthday the other day."

Sofia's mouth fell open, and a chunk of egg threatened to tumble free. "No way. What day?"

"August 17th."

All five of them froze. Then, almost in perfect sync, they all blurted, "That's my birthday too."

The walls echoed with sudden relief, disbelief, and a fragile tendril of hope weaving between them.

Levi stood and shouted toward the ceiling speaker, "We figured it out! We all have the same birthday!"

Bethany pumped her fists, eyes blazing. "So you can let us go now!"

Nothing came from the speaker. No laugh. No taunt. Not even static.

Keisha swallowed a lump of fear. "What if he's dead?"

Paco's eyes widened. "Oh shit..."

Bethany wrapped her arms around herself. "Then we'll be stuck here forever. Oh my God!"

Marcus tore his gaze from the blue hat and fixed them with a flat stare. "This is literally the only reason I wouldn't want that fucker dead."

All five turned to him as though he'd just confessed to some atrocity. Silence collected in their wide eyes.

He blinked, bewildered. "What... you guys disagree?"

Slowly, reluctantly, they shook their heads. He wasn't wrong.

The speaker above them crackled. A warped, sardonic voice seeped through the grille: "Very good."

A lead weight of dread pulsed against their ribs.

"You passed step four," it hissed. "But no, you will not be set free. As you still have not solved it."

Paco jerked his arms skyward. "What the fuck, dude?" He instantly clapped a hand over his mouth. "Sorry!"

Dynamo's laugh slithered into the room... an awful, layered sound that didn't belong to a human. "Well, since Paco wants to be a smart mouth today, we'll change things up for the third test. Instead, he can answer one question."

Paco stiffened, rigid as an iron bar. "And what's that?"

"If you could have a brother or a sister," the voice intoned, cold as a scalpel, "which would it be?"

Paco's brow furrowed; his eyes darted among them like a caged animal fearing the wrong glance. Then he shrugged. "Brother. Totally a bro."

A deafening foghorn blast shook the room.

Everyone jolted. Bethany screamed. Marcus swore. Sofia fell backwards into the wall.

"Wrong answer," Dynamo snarled, voice folding in on itself.

Levi glared up at the speaker. "Why? How? It was a choice!"

Paco stood, shaking with anger and fear. "You asked! I answered! It can't be wrong!"

"Oh," Dynamo drawled, bubbling with glee, "I can make it whatever the hell I want to make it."

The room fell silent.

The moment Dynamo's voice faded, the room felt smaller. Like the walls leaned a fraction closer.

Levi spat a curse, yanking at his ankle chain with white-knuckled fury. Metal snapped against the floor with a harsh ring. "I'm not dying here," he muttered. "I'm not."

Sofia reached for him, only to be yanked away by her own shackle.

Paco pressed his palms to his temples, inhaling ragged breaths that rattled his chest. "He said it was wrong... a choice question. It doesn't even make sense." His voice pitched high enough to shatter glass, and he collapsed to his knees, flattened by invisible pressure.

Keisha wiped her eyes angrily. "I swear to God, if he hurts us because of something stupid like that..." Her voice broke. She pressed her lips together and looked away so no one would see her tears. But Marcus saw them.

Bethany wasn't holding back at all. She sobbed openly on her bed, her head pressed against her knees. "I want to go home," she cried. "I don't want to be here anymore. Please... please..." She wasn't talking to anyone in the room. She was talking to the walls, the ceiling, the invisible man behind the speaker... begging the way a terrified child begs the dark to go away.

"Hey," Marcus said, his voice quieter than he intended. "We're not dead. We need to stay calm and think. That's how we make it out."

Paco let out a bitter laugh. "Okay, Marcus, sure. Let's 'think' our way out of a locked room with metal chains and a sociopath grading our answers like a sadistic teacher."

Keisha wiped her nose with the back of her hand. "He said

we passed step four. That has to mean something. Right?" She glanced at the speaker. "RIGHT?"

Silence.

Sofia stared at the heavy iron link binding her ankle. "What if the next test is worse?" she whispered. "What if he's just warming up?"

A collective shiver raced through them.

Marcus slid his eyes to the ceiling, picturing hidden cameras, Dynamo's grinning face behind the lens. "Whatever he throws at us next," he mumbled, "we face it together."

But even as he spoke, there was a heaviness in his chest. That their matching birthdays and shared captivity weren't coincidences. That something darker tied them together.

Bethany's cries grew more desperate.

Marcus stared at the flimsy birthday hat perched beside his empty plate.

We are so beyond fucked.

CHAPTER 12

DAY FIVE

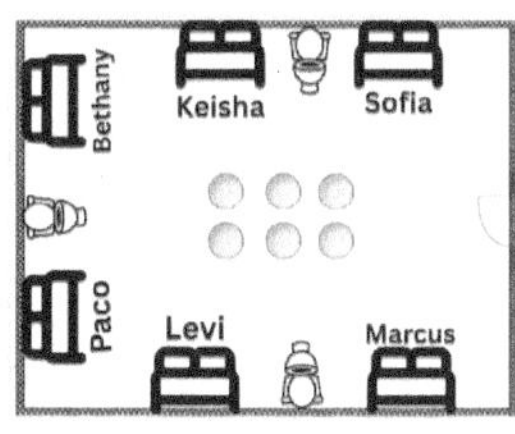

DAY FIVE

The next morning broke under the same merciless glare as the ones before. Harsh white lights snapped on, needles of illumination stabbing every aching muscle. This time, the lights lingered brighter than necessary, as if Dynamo wanted them awake, alert, and uncomfortable. Their nerves rattled like loose screws, bodies stiff with yesterday's aches... but they hauled themselves upright, anyway. Every movement felt negotiated, like their bodies had to be convinced to obey.

Dynamo was ready to play again.

The smell of hot syrup and salty ham curled through the

stale air. It was almost cruel... comforting, familiar, domestic in a place designed to strip those feelings away. Pancakes, browned at the edges, sopped up molten butter; thick-cut ham glistened under the harsh glow. Steam rose lazily from the plates.

Marcus barely noticed the food. A deep, grinding pain throbbed behind his right eye, pulsing in time with his heartbeat. He pressed two fingers to his temple in attempt to stop it.

Leaning against Paco's plate, lay something else: a Nevada license plate, its paint flaking, corners pinched with rust, the numbers half-erased by time.

Paco's fingers hovered above it before he yanked it closer. The metal scraped against the cement with a sound that set everyone on edge. "What the hell is this?"

Sofia leaned closer. "Is that supposed to be the clue?"

Marcus rubbed the bridge of his nose, wincing as his joints cracked. The motion sent a sharp spike of pain through his skull, and he sucked in a breath. "Probably."

Levi ran a hand through his hair. "Paco... you originally from Nevada?"

Paco's brow creased. He turned the plate over, inspecting it. "I don't know."

The silence hummed like an open wound. Even the lights seemed louder.

Keisha's voice fell soft, almost afraid. "What do you mean you don't know?"

He shrugged, trying to shrug off the weight of their stares. "I'm adopted. Was adopted as a baby. My parents told me it was an out-of-country adoption. I never asked what state in the USA. Didn't think it mattered." He laughed, but it cracked and died. "Guess it matters now."

Bethany touched his shoulder. "Then maybe it means nothing. Maybe it's not about where any of us were born."

Lightning seemed to flash behind Sofia's eyes. The realization hit her hard enough to make her sit straighter. "I was born in Nevada."

Keisha's chest heaved. Her breath came shallow. "Oh my God... me too."

Levi dropped his fork. It clattered loudly against the plate. "Holy shit. I think that is where I was born, too."

Bethany joined in. "I was born in Colorado, as far as I know."

Marcus exhaled, eyes darting between them. He felt the pattern snapping into place like a trap closing. "Paco... except for you and Bethany... all of us were born in Nevada."

Paco blinked. "What?"

Sofia nodded. "I grew up in Florida, but I was born in Nevada."

Paco stared down at the plate, the room suddenly unbearably small. "So this... could be about me. Or it could be about all of you."

The speaker on the far wall sparked to life, an oily whisper in the cool air. Static crackled first, like a throat clearing.

"Well done," Dynamo's voice slithered out, lower now, stripped of its earlier warmth, each word carefully sharpened. "You're finally using those beautiful brains I've invested so much time into."

Bethany flinched at the word invested, as if it tasted like poisoned candy. Her hand curled into a fist.

Marcus crossed his arms. His vision blurred slightly, the pain now impossible to ignore. "Before we do anything else..." He swallowed. "I need something for my head. A painkiller. Please." It was instinct more than defiance.

There was a pause. A long one.

Then Dynamo laughed. "Oh, Marcus," Dynamo crooned. "No."

Marcus stiffened. "What?"

"No painkillers," Dynamo continued smoothly. "Pain

dulls when treated. And dull minds make poor choices." A faint hum rolled through the walls. "You don't need relief. You need to feel."

Keisha's voice trembled. "He's hurting."

"Yes," Dynamo agreed softly. "And that is the point."

Marcus clenched his teeth as another wave of pain crashed through him. "What's the test today?"

A low hum began, like hidden turbines stuttering to life within the walls.

Dynamo chuckled again. "A simple exercise in honesty and identity. I will ask each of you one question about who you are."

A metal slot slid open with a pneumatic hiss, revealing six pale cards, each bearing a single name:

Marcus

Keisha

Sofia

Levi

Bethany
Paco

They stared at the names as if they might bite.

"Take your card," Dynamo instructed, voice cool as steel. "But don't look at it yet."

Their hands hovered, then closed over the cards. Hearts pounded in unison.

Dynamo continued, "Read aloud the statement on the back. The others will decide whether it fits the person named."

Cold dread spilled through them. No one wanted to be seen this clearly.

"Begin," Dynamo demanded.

Marcus flipped his card with trembling fingers. His voice cracked as he read: "Marcus is the type of man who holds on to guilt until it crushes him."

His throat tightened. No one spoke. Then Levi nodded. "True."

Soft agreements rippled around the room.

Keisha's turn. "Keisha always blames herself first, even when she shouldn't."

Sofia's nod was immediate. "True."

Keisha felt tears pooling, but she stayed silent. She pressed her lips together until the feeling passed.

"Sofia hides fear by pretending she's irritated."

They all chuckled nervously, and the word "True" was spat out in unison.

Levi's hands shook as he turned his card. "Levi gets angry

when he feels helpless."

Keisha didn't hesitate. "True."

Levi's eyes went to the floor.

Bethany read hers slowly. "Bethany is terrified of being forgotten."

They agreed.

Then it was Paco's turn.

Hands shaking, he flipped the card. His voice wavered as he read: "Paco believes he doesn't belong anywhere."

Silence fell like concrete. Paco closed his eyes. The words felt carved into him.

Keisha spoke first, carefully. "True."

Sofia's nod felt like a verdict. "Yeah."

Levi swallowed thickly. "Same."

Bethany's whisper cut through the stillness: "I'm sorry."

Marcus met Paco's gaze, fierce and gentle. "It's true. But that doesn't mean it has to stay true."

The speaker sputtered once more.

"Well done," Dynamo intoned, almost tender. "You've passed today's test. Consider me... impressed. Today's lesson: acceptance."

A tremor of relief washed through them, as if they'd nearly drowned and were at last breathing again.

But before they could savor it, Dynamo's voice drifted back, softer, darker:

"Enjoy the victory," he drawled. "It may be your last."

CHAPTER 13

DAY SIX

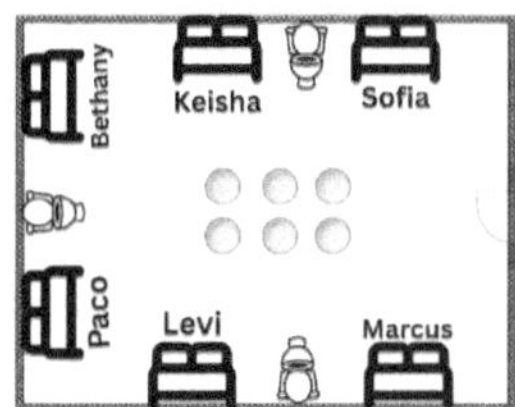

A blue stethoscope.

Bethany stared at it, her mouth tightening until her lips nearly disappeared. "What does this have to do with anything?" Her voice echoed off the bare walls, bouncing back at them like a taunt.

Paco leaned in, the chain at his ankle scraping against the floor as he picked up the stethoscope and tried it out. "Damn, it's real." The rubber felt tacky against his skin.

Keisha frowned, sweat beading along her hairline despite the goosebumps on her arms. "First a photo, then the birthday hat, Nevada license plate, and now this stethoscope.

What's the connection with all of these?"

Sofia chewed her thumbnail until she tasted blood. "No idea."

Marcus asked, his voice tight with thirst, "Does anyone know a doctor?"

Heads shook in the oppressive silence.

"Anyone have a doctor in the family?" Keisha tried shifting her weight to relieve the pressure of the metal cuff digging into her ankle.

Bethany hesitated, her eyes darting to the ceiling. "My mom's not a doctor," she said slowly, each word measured. "She's an ultrasound tech."

They all stared at her expectantly, the air between them thick with desperation.

She shrugged weakly, shoulders hunched against the weight of their collective hope. "Maybe that's it? I dunno."

Silence followed, broken only by the distant drip of water somewhere beyond their prison.

No voice came over the speaker. No mechanical hum acknowledging success. Just the sound of their own ragged breathing and pounding hearts.

Levi scratched his neck, leaving angry red welts. "Well... it has to be something to do with a hospital. Or medicine. Or whatever."

The speaker crackled violently, making Bethany jump. Her chain jangled, a discordant note in their symphony of fear.

"That," Dynamo said, his tone smooth and pleased, slithering into the room like toxic mist, "is correct."

The group collectively exhaled, some in relief, some in dread.

"What's the test this time?" Marcus asked stiffly, muscles coiled tight beneath his sweat-stained shirt.

"Oh," Dynamo purred, the sound seeming to come from everywhere at once, "this one's about perception. About seeing things that aren't there... and believing things you shouldn't."

Levi muttered, his words falling like stones. "So... illusions."

"Exactly."

But Dynamo didn't begin... not yet.

The speaker fell silent, the lights dimmed until shadows pooled in the corners like liquid, and for a few minutes they did nothing but wait in uneasy quiet.

Bethany sank down against the far wall, the concrete cold enough to seep through her clothes. Paco moved with her, sitting as close as their chains allowed... only a few inches apart.

"You okay?" Paco asked gently, his eyes reflecting what little light remained.

She shook her head, a strand of hair sticking to her tear-dampened cheek. "My parents recently got divorced. I've been struggling with it." Her voice was small in the vastness of their cell.

"Damn, I'm sorry," he replied, his fingers inching toward hers on the gritty floor.

"I took out my anger on both of them. It felt like they broke something inside me." Her shoulders shook as if the words themselves were punches to her chest. "Now, I would give anything to see them again. I've realized... the idea of never seeing my parents, it's far worse than being split between two separate homes."

Paco reached over, fingertips cool against her shoulder. "You have every right to be angry. Divorce rips your world apart. It takes time to learn how to breathe again."

Bethany stared at the concrete floor, her legs pulled in close.

"I was getting too depressed about it. So my friends made me a dating profile." She forced a laugh. "Like that was gonna fix everything."

Paco offered a gentle smile. "Did it?"

"No. I freaked out. Yelled at them. Had a huge fight with my best friend the last time I saw her." Bethany finally looked up, her lashes glistening. "What if she hates me now?"

Paco grabbed her hand. "If she's your best friend, she doesn't hate you. She's probably missing you like crazy."

Bethany blinked back tears, clinging to his reassurance. "Thanks."

A few feet away, Marcus and Levi talked quietly.

"Man," Marcus sighed, pressing a palm to the wall as if he could feel its pulse, "I'd kill for a basketball right now."

Levi laughed under his breath. "Dude, same. A game of Horse sounds great right about now."

Marcus's eyebrows shot up. "What position do you play?" Marcus asked, tone sharper than before.

"Shooting guard," Levi said proudly. "Deadly from the corner."

Marcus let out a low whistle. "Bet I could take you."

Levi scoffed, rolling his shoulders. "Nah. You'd foul out before you could."

"Favorite NBA team?" Marcus pressed.

Levi's grin flickered in the half-light. "Lakers, of course."

Marcus nodded, exhaling a cloud of tension. "They were mine too. Now... I'm stuck rooting for the Knicks."

The banter, brief and warm, broke some of the tension.

On the opposite side, Keisha leaned back against the wall, rubbing her temples as if the pain could be scrubbed away. "I'm probably fired by now. I hated being a waitress, but still... losing it would suck."

Sofia tucked a stray strand of hair behind her ear. "I'm a lifeguard. I guess that's ironic now, huh? Can't save anybody in here."

Keisha gave a tired laugh. "If we make it out, I swear I'll never complain about rude customers again."

Sofia nodded, shoulders sagging. "Same."

Keisha looked at her. "You got a boyfriend waiting?"

Sofia laughed, shaking her head. "No time for that right now. I'm focusing on me first."

"I like that," Keisha said softly.

"You?"

"Not anyone exclusively. Dating around, seeing my options."

"Fair enough," Sofia responds.

They sat with that for a moment, a fragile sense of connection forming between them all.

Suddenly the overhead lights exploded into chaotic strobing. The sterile white cut down to a jaundiced yellow that dripped across the walls. Dynamo's voice slid back in.

"Step six begins now."

The surrounding walls shimmered... literally shimmered, like heat waves rising from asphalt. The air thickened. Shadows stretched and twisted, pulling long across the floor.

Sofia gasped. "What the..."

Flickering on the walls: haunted hospital corridors, iron gurneys wheeling themselves toward them, surgeons in blood-smeared gowns with featureless faces.

Bethany clamped her hands over her eyes. "Oh my God!"

"This is not real. None of it is. But you must prove you believe that," Dynamo crooned.

Marcus seized the cold steel chain dangling at his side. "It's all hallucination," he spat.

The images intensified... cadavers rising, fingers clawing at their ankles, the ceiling bowing like a monstrous presence overhead.

Levi roared, "He's trying to make us freak out!"

Sofia pressed her palms into her ears, rocking gently. "It feels so real!"

Keisha forced herself onto her knees, every breath rallying her will. "It isn't. Think of it like virtual reality."

"Exactly," Marcus cut in. "Count something real. Anything."

Bethany whispered, her voice cracking, "The chains. They're real."

Paco pressed his palm against his sternum, feeling each thunderous beat. "My heartbeat. That's real." Sweat trickled down his temple.

"I hear your voice," Sofia said, her eyes darting frantically between shadows that stretched like fingers across the floor.

Keisha pinched her own arm until white marks bloomed red. "I feel pain. That's real."

Marcus took a deep breath, nostrils flaring as he stared at the hallucinations crawling over the walls. "These images aren't real. We already know this." His voice trembled. "Did we pass or fail?"

The illusions pulsed in response, warping, distorting, the colors bleeding into impossible hues that hurt to look at.

"Louder," Dynamo hissed through the speakers, the sound scraping against their eardrums.

Marcus shouted, veins bulging in his neck, "THIS ISN'T REAL!"

Bethany yelled, tears streaming down her face, "IT'S FAKE!"

Sofia screamed until her throat burned, "YOU CAN'T

TRICK US!"

"Then why are you flinching away from them?" Dynamo's voice slithered into their minds. "LOOK! Beyond the images, really look."

They forced themselves still, muscles quivering with effort. After a few moments of refusing to show fear, the images rippled like torn cloth, and then shattered with the sound of breaking glass.

The room snapped back to its plain gray walls. The air cleared, cool against their feverish skin. The lights steadied to a harsh fluorescent glare.

Dynamo chuckled, the sound intimate as if whispered directly into their ears. "Well done. You passed step six."

They slumped in relief.

"But don't get comfortable," Dynamo added lightly, a smile evident in the voice. "An illusion is a difficult thing to break... especially when it is right in front of you."

The speaker clicked off with finality.

CHAPTER 14

DAY SEVEN

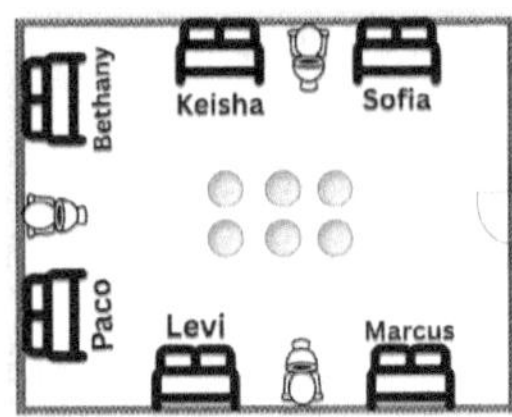

A glossy ultrasound photo rested beside Keisha's plate this morning. It was positioned too neatly, like someone knew exactly whose eyes it would snag first.

The sight of it hit differently today. The stale air was heavy with the smell of unwashed skin, damp clothes, and the faint metallic tang of stress-sweat. Everyone kept catching themselves sniffing their own shirts, grimacing, pretending they weren't doing it. The awareness of their own bodies had become impossible to ignore... greasy hair, sticky skin, mouths that tasted sour no matter how much water they drank. They all wanted a shower.

God, they needed one, but wanting didn't matter in this place.

Levi was the first to speak, rubbing sleep from his eyes, his hair sticking up in wild greasy tufts. He squinted at the photo like it might change if he blinked hard enough. "What did you get?"

Keisha frowned, picking up the picture. Her fingers trembled slightly, and she adjusted her grip so no one would notice. She turned it over, scanning the printed date in the corner, then her mother's name written in official block letters. Her breath caught.

"It's an ultrasound photo of me," she said. Her voice came out thin. She cleared her throat and tried again, but the weakness stayed.

The others gathered around her. Sofia scooted closer, trying to ignore the way her shirt stuck to her back. Marcus leaned in as near as he could. His jaw flexed as if he were bracing for impact. Bethany took the photo when Keisha offered it, her brows knitting.

"Aww, you were so…" Bethany murmured. She flipped the picture gently, studying the shape inside the murky gray. But then her expression changed. Her eyes widened, almost comically large, except nothing was funny here.

"Wait," she drawled slowly. "This... this is for sure you?"

Keisha's stomach pulled tight. A cold, crawling sensation settled just under her ribs. "Yeah. Why? What's wrong?"

Bethany looked up gradually, as though afraid to say it. "This is a boy."

Keisha blinked. Her mind refused to connect the words to meaning. "No. No way. How would you even know that? It's just a blob."

Bethany shook her head. Her grip tightened on the photo until her knuckles whitened. "My mom's an ultrasound tech. She taught me how to tell the difference. And this fetus is definitely a boy."

Marcus threw his hands up. The movement was sharp, agitated, like he was trying to shake the thought loose. "Are you fucking with us right now?"

"No," Bethany said, clutching the photo like it might shatter. "I'm serious. Your mom was carrying a boy."

The overhead speaker crackled violently. Everyone flinched as if struck. Sofia dropped her spoon. Marcus grabbed Levi's shoulder instinctively. Paco cursed under his breath.

Then came Dynamo's voice... smooth, smug, and delighted. There was a smile in it they couldn't see but could feel, like fingers pressing into a bruise. "Now... now... it's about time you started *figuring shit out.*"

Levi yelled toward the ceiling. His voice broke halfway through the shout. "What does that mean?!"

"It means," Dynamo replied, "that if you ever want to leave this place, you should start putting the clues together. No test today. You have the day to talk. To think. You aren't the only ones who want this over." The implication lingered, ugly and deliberate.

The speaker clicked off, leaving a hum of static in its place. The silence afterward felt heavier than the noise had.

For a long moment, nobody moved.

Then everything erupted at once.

Sofia burst into tears first, covering her mouth as if she could hide the sound. Marcus swore and kicked the leg of one of the bunks hard enough to make the metal ring. He winced but didn't stop. Levi was mumbling something to himself. Over and over, like a mantra gone wrong. Bethany sat frozen, as if afraid moving would make any of this more real. Paco rubbed his face with both hands, trying to breathe. Keisha stayed perfectly still, her hands curled in her lap.

They ate their food and gathered in a circle on the cold floor. No one commented on how little anyone actually ate. The ultrasound photo lay in the middle like the center of a ritual. No one wanted to touch it again, but no one wanted to look away either.

Sofia hugged her knees. "Okay... the clues we have so far: the Nevada license plate. The stethoscope. Sofia's brother's obituary. And now, Keisha's ultrasound."

"And we all share the same birthday," Marcus added. He rubbed his face hard, as if exhaustion might peel off with skin. "Which is weird. Like government-lab weirdness."

Keisha rubbed her temples. "My mom always told me I was her miracle baby. But she never mentioned... anything like this."

"Why would she hide something that huge?" Sofia asked gently. Her eyes stayed locked on Keisha's face.

Keisha didn't have an answer.

Paco shifted closer to Bethany, his leg rubbing hers. She didn't pull away. Instead, she moved her leg closer, staring at the photo as though trying to solve a puzzle that refused to be solved. The contact seemed to steady them both, just a little.

"It doesn't mean she lied," Bethany said softly. "Sometimes parents don't know how to talk about painful things. Or maybe she didn't know."

Paco nodded. His voice came out rough. "Yeah. Or maybe someone else did something."

Bethany looked at him, her eyes shimmering. "Are you implying what I think you are?"

"I don't want to think that," Paco said. "But what if this nutcase is right? What if all of this is connected?"

The group fell silent again. The idea settled over them like a weight they couldn't shrug off.

Marcus stood up, pacing the floor, running a hand through his hair. "Nevada plate. Stethoscope. Shared birthday. A boy-in-utero who became Keisha. Sofia's brother's obituary. What the hell ties all that together?" He groaned and continued, "I need a fucking smoke."

Sofia swallowed. "Me too."

Bethany rubbed at her eyes, smearing tears across her cheeks. Levi kept digging at the dirt under his nails as if trying to scrape himself clean. Paco pressed his forehead against his knees at one point, breathing hard. The stress, the smell, the claustrophobia... they were all fraying at the same thread. Their bodies ached. Their minds felt stretched thin, as if Dynamo were pulling them apart fiber by fiber.

Levi finally said, his voice hoarse, almost afraid of being right, "Something must have happened in Nevada at the hospital on our birthday."

"Something involving us," Bethany added, glancing at

Keisha.

They tossed around many ideas. As the day passed, their theories spiraled, tangled, grew, collapsed. Hope flared and died over and over. They talked in circles, argued, apologized, and kept going. The weight of the clues pressed on all of them, but the uncertainty pressed even harder.

At some point, Paco sat beside Bethany again. He didn't make a move; he just stayed near her, his knee brushing hers. She leaned into him, her breath hitching once before she caught it.

Across the room, Keisha watched them with a small, distant smile before returning to the ultrasound photo. It felt alien in her hands now. Her thumb traced the image... this strange, impossible version of who she was supposed to be.

"I don't get it," she whispered. "If my mom was carrying a boy... then how the hell did she end up with me?"

No one answered.

But the question hung with them all, heavy and impossible, as the hours slipped away in their locked cell and the shadows grew long on the concrete floor.

Dynamo didn't speak again.

He didn't need to.

The clues were finally working.

CHAPTER 15

DAY EIGHT

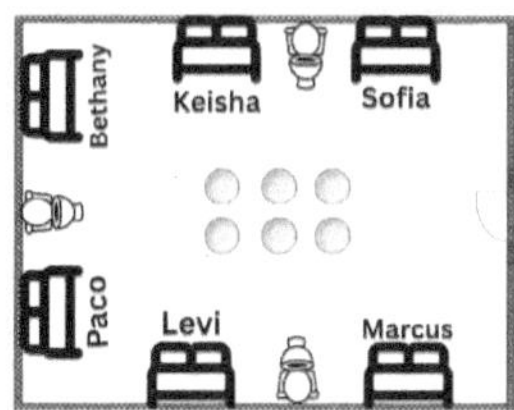

This time there were no cryptic notes or puzzling objects by their plates of lukewarm oatmeal. No one said a word while eating, but the slump of their shoulders and the mechanical way they spooned food into their mouths told the same story. They were utterly defeated.

The metal slot in the door suddenly clanked open with a harsh metallic screech. Everyone froze mid-motion. Even Paco's spoon stopped halfway to his mouth.

A claw like grabber slid through the narrow opening, holding something, and dropped it in the middle of the floor with a soft slap. A cream-colored envelope with Levi's name scrawled in elegant black cursive.

No one moved at first, as if the envelope might explode. Then Levi leaned forward, his chain scraping along the concrete floor like nails on a chalkboard as he pulled the envelope closer with trembling fingers. He turned it over in his hands, examining the unmarked seal.

"That is new," Keisha muttered, her eyes narrowed suspiciously.

"Open it," Sofia said, leaning forward until her chain pulled taut.

Levi hesitated only a moment before tearing it open with his thumbnail. Glossy photographs spilled out onto the concrete floor.

Everyone leaned in to look.

It was a bunch of family photos.

Birthday parties. School pictures with awkward smiles and outdated haircuts. Cheap drugstore prints mixed with what looked like scanned copies of older, sepia-toned ones.

"That's my mom," Levi said immediately, grabbing one with shaking hands. "That's my house."

Paco snatched another, his eyebrows knitting together. "So the clue is your family? Why?"

Marcus grabbed one next, frowning hard enough to deepen

the lines around his mouth. "This is weird. Really fucking weird."

Bethany reached for one near the edge of the pile. It showed a family of four standing in front of a bungalow-style house painted a cheerful periwinkle blue. A tall man with broad shoulders and a woman with reddish-brown hair stood close together with two children, all smiling at the camera as if they didn't have a care in the world.

Bethany stared at it, her breath snagging in her throat.

The girl looked about eight years old. Coppery hair that caught the light just like Bethany's used to. The same button nose with a spray of freckles. The same wide-set blue eyes. But the family wasn't hers. She had never seen them before in her life. Her stomach twisted into a cold, tight knot.

"This is you and your family?" she questioned, waving the photo at Levi.

Levi looked the photo over. "Yeah. My parents and my little sister."

"Your sister looks so much like me," she said, tracing the girl's face with her fingertip. "So do your parents."

"Now that you say that, they kind of do, but they are gingers. I'm the only brunette in the family," Levi said, running his hand through his greasy chestnut hair.

She picked up another photo with shaking hands, a glossy 5x7. "How is this possible?" she whispered to herself. She looked at Levi, her eyes wide with panic. "You don't see what I see. I'm a natural ginger. I just dye my hair this color."

"Are you serious?" he asks, leaning in closer.

"I dye my hair so I fit in with my family better," she states, tugging at her dark ponytail. "None of them are ginger, other than my grandmother."

Paco started flipping through the photos faster, his dirty fingers smudging the glossy surfaces. "Oh, hell no," he muttered, sweat beading on his upper lip. "You can't... what does this all mean?"

They spread the photos out across the floor, forming a messy collage of mismatched families and familiar faces in unfamiliar places.

Above them, the speaker crackled like bacon in a hot pan. Everyone jumped. They all cranked their necks toward the ceiling.

Waiting for Dynamo's raspy voice.

Waiting for the next cryptic clue.

But no words came. Just static, like the sound of rain on an empty highway.

And then silence.

For the first time since they arrived in this claustrophobic prison, Dynamo said nothing at all. And somehow, that was worse than anything he could say.

They spent the rest of the day hunched over the photographs, trying to piece together what it all means. They had one guess when it came to Levi and Bethany, but it sounded crazy even to their own ears.

Dynamo announced it was time for bed like every other night, his voice finally returning through the speakers like a ghost. He said that they were finally ready, and the answer would be revealed tomorrow, when the morning light would expose the truth they weren't prepared to face.

CHAPTER 16

DAY NINE

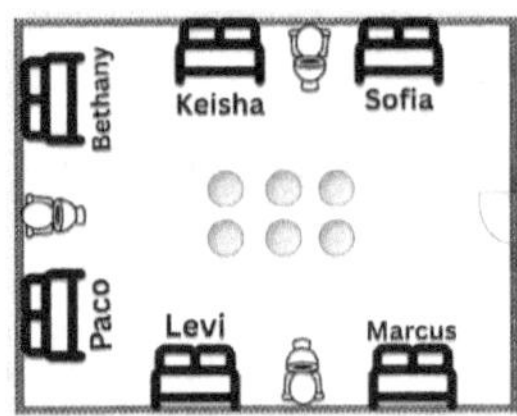

By now, none of them trusted the idea of time anymore. The room never changed. The air never changed. The buzzing lights and gray concrete walls stayed exactly the same, pressing in on them day after day. But something had changed. Something among the group. Reality was starting to crash against logic like waves against jagged rocks.

Bethany stared at the photographs still scattered across the floor. None of them had bothered to put them away. It felt wrong to touch them too much, as if moving them might somehow make everything worse, as if they were cursed objects from another life.

Levi sat with his back against the wall, one knee drawn up, his fingers drumming a nervous staccato rhythm against his leg. He kept glancing at the door, its surface scratched and dented from previous occupants.

Marcus paced as far as his chain would allow, turning sharply every few steps.

Keisha sat cross-legged, picking at a loose teal thread on her fraying sleeve until it unraveled into a small pile on the floor.

Sofia leaned against the wall with her eyes closed, though she clearly wasn't asleep.

Paco lay flat on his back, arms spread like a fallen angel, staring up at the water-stained ceiling tiles as if they might reveal answers in their mottled patterns.

None of them talked much anymore. The silence hung thick as fog. They were all thinking the same thing; the thought pulsing between them like an electric current. Something big was coming.

The metal slot in the door clanked open.

Everyone jolted.

The claw delivered a stack of envelopes this time. Six of them. One for each of them, each name typed in perfect black letters.

No one moved at first.

Then Marcus said, "We better open them."

Bethany grabbed hers first. Her hands were already shaking before she even touched it.

"Three," Paco said suddenly, his voice echoing in the concrete chamber.

Everyone looked at him, faces pale and drawn in the harsh light.

"We open them on three."

No one argued. Six pairs of eyes locked onto six identical envelopes.

"One," he said, the word hanging heavy in the air.

Bethany's fingers slipped under the flap, the paper's edge sharp against her skin.

"Two."

She felt as if she might throw up.

"Three."

Six envelopes tore open at once, the sound like fabric ripping.

Papers slid out, crisp and official.

Official papers with government letterheads and watermarks catching the harsh light.

DNA REPORTS

Their stomachs dropped.

"What the..." Keisha groaned, her voice cracking like thin ice.

Bethany's trembling fingers clutched the edges of the paper as her eyes crawled down the page, each word hitting her like a physical blow.

Test Subject: Bethany Taylor

Mother: Lisa Tucker
Father: Brent Tucker

Her brain stalled, thoughts colliding like derailed trains.

Those weren't even remotely close to her parents' names.

Across from her, Paco made a strangled noise, like someone had punched him in the throat. His caramel skin had taken on an ashen hue.

"What the hell?" he rasped.

Keisha stared at her paper, her face draining of color. "No... no, that's not right." Her fingers pressed against her lips as if physically holding back a scream.

Marcus flipped his page over to look at the back. "This is fake. This has to be fake."

Levi hadn't said anything. Bethany looked at him. His paper trembled in his hands, and his knuckles were bleached white with tension.

"What does yours say?" she asked, her voice sounding foreign to her own ears.

He didn't answer, just stared at the paper as if it might burst into flames.

Bethany leaned forward as far as she could.

"Levi," she groaned.

Slowly, he turned the paper toward her, revealing the truth in stark black and white.

Test Subject: Amber Tucker

Mother: Lauren Taylor
Father: Travis Taylor

Bethany stopped breathing. The room tilted sideways, then righted itself with nauseating suddenness.

Those were her parents.

"No," she moaned, the sound wrenched from somewhere deep and primal.

Her hands shook violently as she looked back down at her own paper. Then back at Levi's. And back at hers again, as if the words might rearrange themselves into something that made sense.

Her vision blurred, the words swimming before her like fish in murky water.

"That's... that's not possible." Each word felt like glass in her throat.

Keisha suddenly spoke, her voice cutting through the fog. "Who are the parents on yours?" Her dark eyes were intense.

Bethany swallowed the desert in her mouth. "The... the Tuckers."

Levi gasped. "Lisa and Brent?" he said hesitantly, his voice small and lost like a child's.

The blood drained from her face as she responded, "Yeah," her eyes growing wider with each passing second.

Paco went still, his shoulders tensing beneath his sweat-stained t-shirt. "My paper says Lopez."

Silence fell like a concrete slab, crushing the oxygen out of the room.

Sofia looked up slowly, her dark lashes wet with unshed tears. "Allison and Leroy?"

Paco nodded to confirm.

A single tear carved a glistening path down Sofia's olive cheek. "Those are my parents."

"But your brother passed awa..." Paco trailed off, his voice cracking. His chest constricted as if invisible hands were squeezing his lungs. Was it possible that he was her brother?

No one moved. Realization spread through them slowly. Like cold water rising. Each of them clutched a paper bearing the devastating truth: they were biologically the children of the other's parents.

Connected by an invisible thread that made their stomachs churn with nausea.

Bethany's thoughts raced.

Same birthday.

Same state.

The ultrasound showing a boy.

The obituary.

The photographs.

"No way. It can't be possible. Were we switched at birth?" Bethany questioned.

No one reacted at first; their faces frozen in various stages of horror.

Marcus shook his head, his dark curls catching the light. "No. That isn't possible, is it? That would mean that I was the baby in the..."

Keisha mumbles in a scared tone, "Ultrasound."

After all, the names on his paper were Keisha's parents, and it was his parents on hers.

"Yes," Bethany said, louder now, her fists clenched until her knuckles whitened. "That's the only thing that makes fucking sense."

Sofia covered her mouth, her silver ring catching the light.

Paco stared at the floor, speechless.

Keisha's eyes filled with tears that clung to her lashes before spilling down her cheeks.

Levi just sat there, unmoving.

"You're telling me," Marcus said slowly, each word deliberate and heavy, "we all ended up in the wrong families?"

Bethany shook her head. "Not ended up," she answered, her voice cold as steel. "Put."

The word hung in the air like poisonous gas.

Put.

Above them, the speaker came on. They all stared up at it, waiting for Dynamo's voice. For confirmation or denial.

But no voice came.

Instead... a small metallic clang echoed through the room, reverberating off the bare walls.

Something small and brass hit the floor, spinning twice before settling.

A key.

It lay in the center of the room, glinting under the harsh light.

No one moved.

Then Paco's voice cut through the silence, "Is this a fucking joke?" His words vibrated with barely contained rage.

Marcus lunged forward, snatching the key between his long fingers. “It’s real,” he said, turning it over, examining the worn teeth and scratched surface.

One by one, they maneuvered closer, forming a tight circle of desperate hope.

Marcus tried it on his ankle cuff. The lock clicked open.

They passed it around, undoing all of their cuffs, the sound of each release like a promise of freedom they weren’t sure they wanted anymore.

Finally, all six of them were free. They stood there for a moment, rubbing their swollen ankles, staring at each other in disbelief.

“We can leave?” Sofia asked in shock.

Marcus limped to the metal door, his palm leaving a sweaty print on the surface as he tried the handle. It was still locked. He rattled it harder. It didn’t budge.

Paco laughed weakly. “Of course, we are still trapped.”

Bethany sank back against the wall, her unwashed hair catching on the rough surface. “What now?”

No one had an answer.

And Dynamo never spoke again.

They spent one more day in that room.

One long, endless day.

No food came this time. Their stomachs twisted into painful knots.

No more clues. Just silence, and the truth sitting heavy between them like a seventh prisoner.

Until finally... footsteps echoed beyond the door. Not shuffling or dragging, but purposeful.

Real footsteps.

Marcus shot to his feet. "Do you hear that?"

Everyone stood, their muscles tensed like cornered animals.

Someone was trying to get the door open from the other side.

The lock snapped, and the door burst open. Light flooded the room, blinding and overwhelming. Two figures stood in the doorway.

"Police!" one of them shouted, the word bouncing off the walls.

Bethany covered her eyes. The light hurt. Every inch of her body throbbed with a dull, persistent ache.

"It's okay," the other voice said, soft and unfamiliar. "You're safe now."

"We have looked for you for days," said one of the officers.

Safe.

The word hung in the air like a foreign language they had

forgotten how to speak.

One of the officers stepped forward, his badge catching the merciless light.

"We're Detectives Riley and Reed," he said gently, his weathered face creased with concern. "You're going home."

Keisha looked back at the others, their hollow faces mirroring her own exhaustion and confusion.

They all had the same thought, reflected in their vacant stares.

Which home?

One by one, the six of them stepped out of the building that had held them for days, for what felt like a lifetime, their shoulders hunched beneath the weight of a truth none of them had asked for.

CHAPTER 17

CALEB

The projector flickers off behind me, the last slide of my presentation casting a faint afterglow across the classroom. For half a second, the room is still tinted blue, like the past refuses to fully let go. I step away from the podium, letting the silence linger just long enough for the weight of the story to settle in. The class has been quiet—not out of disinterest, but reverence. Sometimes, silence says more than questions ever could.

I lean back against the wall and look out at the faces staring at me. Mostly young and idealistic. They still believe the world makes sense. The bad guys look like bad guys. That help never comes with a price. They are trying to piece together the madness I had just unraveled over the last three hours.

"Alright," I say, clasping my hands. My palms are damp,

and I wipe them subtly against my pants. “Questions?”

A girl in the front with a blue butterfly clip in her hair raises her hand slowly, hesitantly. “So... was that really the truth?”

I nod once.

“Yes,” I answer. “They were all switched at birth.”

"So the ultrasound photo was Marcus?" she probes.

"Yes, it was Marcus in that photo. He was switched with Keisha. Paco was switched with the boy who died, so he's actually Sofia's twin brother, and Bethany and Levi were switched."

A few students shift in their seats.

“It wasn’t just some story or theory,” I continue. “The DNA confirmed it. Each of them went home to the wrong family from the hospital, except for Sofia.” I pause, choosing my words carefully. “They had a lot to work through after that. The kids. The parents. Everyone involved did.” I exhale slowly. “It was a complete mess.”

A girl in the second row raises her hand. “What happened to the kids?”

I nod, the question expected, but still hard to answer. I take a deep breath, sorting through the timeline in my head, through faces that never quite leave me alone.

“Well,” I begin, “as far as I know, Paco Garcia is up in

British Columbia. He's doing well. Found peace, I think, or at least something close to it."

I pause, watching their pens scribble.

"Keisha Williams got married a few years back."

A few students nodded silently.

"Marcus Davis..." I trail off, a flicker of something bitter twisting in my stomach. "He recently rescued his sister from the same crooked organization that got us tangled up in the first place. Other than that, I don't know much about him."

I could feel their curiosity sharpen with each name.

"Levi Tucker has become some kind of social media guru. Influencer with money. He's also married now."

Levi reinvented himself better than any of us. Or maybe he just learned how to hide it better.

"And Sofia?" someone asked.

I shook my head. "Not sure what happened to Sofia. She ghosted after everything went down. Maybe that was the smartest move any of us made." Disappear before the past can drag you back under. I don't blame her.

A long silence follows, as if everyone knows what's coming. Even after all these years, I still dread this part.

"And Bethany Taylor..." I exhale slowly, locking eyes with no one. My throat tightens. "Bethany got caught in the crossfire during the takedown. She was trying to help, to do the right thing. But the wrong day, wrong time. She was murdered a couple of years after this all took place."

I cross my arms and look down. I see her smile instead of the blood. I choose to keep it that way. "God rest her soul."

The classroom is silent. Not the uneasy kind; this is heavier. A moment of collective grief, even from those who never knew her. That's the strange power of stories. Pain travels.

Then, a hand in the back peeks over the crowd. "Do you think... the guy who took them... do you think he was trying to help them? Or was he just hurting people?"

I let that one hang in the air for a second, because I've asked myself that question more nights than I can count.

"My opinion?" I say, my voice low. "I think he believed he was helping. In his mind, he saw himself as some kind of protector, trying to open their eyes to the bigger picture. Show them the corruption, the lies, the things no one else dared to say out loud. But his methods..." I shake my head. "He had a *really shitty* way of doing it."

I look around the room one last time, scanning faces I probably won't see again.

"That's the thing about justifying pain in the name of truth," I say, standing up straighter. "It usually ends with more pain than truth."

"How did you find them?" one of the students asks.

"I received an anonymous phone call that morning. I think it was from him. He told me where they were being kept, and where the key was for the door," I answer, thinking back to that phone call.

A few gasp in shock. Some nod. No one says anything for a moment, then someone quietly closes their notebook.

The sound feels final.

"Alright," I announce, tapping my watch. "That's it for me. Thanks for listening. I know this wasn't the usual lesson plan."

The class murmurs their goodbyes and starts filtering out. I stay behind to gather my things. Backpack. Notes. That old picture of the six of them that I keep folded in my wallet. I hesitate before tucking it away again.

When I step outside, my truck is parked two blocks down, and I take my time walking to it, letting the unusually cool air steady me. I'm not in a rush to get back to the chaotic life I seem to live.

***

As I pull up to my house, I see someone sitting on my steps. A vehicle I don't recognize is parked out front. I kill the engine and sit there longer than I should, listening to the faint ticking of the cooling motor.

The man is sitting with his legs stretched out, resting his elbows on his knees, and has his hoodie pulled over his head. He doesn't look up right away. Just sits there with his head down, as if he's been waiting a long time.

Recognition doesn't hit all at once. It creeps in. My stomach drops as my brain starts catching up with my gut.

I did not expect this today.

Stepping out of the truck, I take a few slow steps forward, every one of them dragging years behind it.

"Lee?" I call out, unsure if my eyes are lying.

His name feels dangerous in my mouth. Like saying it too loudly might undo the miracle.

He looks up. His eyes are sunken in, as if he hasn't slept in days.

"Hey, brother," he answers.

Those two words make my chest cave in. For three decades, the word "brother" belonged to the past tense. To unanswered questions and grief that never got to finish its job.

Every part of me is afraid that if I blink, he'll be gone again.

And just like that, the past comes crashing back. Not

through memory, not through lectures or slides, but through reality, standing on my doorstep.

CHAPTER 18

CALEB

Lee's sitting there like a ghost from another life—solid, real, but somehow still hard to believe.

I slow my steps, taking him in. Thirty years missing, and now he's just... here. And I don't know whether to grab him or keep my distance. I walk up and sit beside him. The position feels familiar in a way that makes my chest ache. I remember sitting here with Cassidy, telling her we'd be okay when I wasn't sure I believed it myself.

Through the window, I catch movement. Cass peeks out from behind the curtain. She gives me a small wave, careful not to draw attention. Like she's afraid she'll scare him off. I raise my hand and wave back. Reassurance without words.

Then I turn to Lee. He's still staring ahead.

"What's going on?" I ask gently. "What brings you here?"

He doesn't answer right away. His eyes drift to my truck

like it's safer than looking at me. I wonder how many times he's rehearsed this moment in his head.

"Nicole told me where you lived," he says finally. "Cassidy told me what time you usually get home. Offered to let me wait inside, but..."

He shrugs, a tight, awkward movement.

"I don't feel comfortable in your home quite yet."

The honesty stings, but I respect it. It hurts to realize my home isn't safe to him yet, but then again, nothing probably is.

I sway my head up and down. "Fair enough."

He shifts beside me, tugging at the cuffs of his hoodie, fingers worrying the fabric like it's the only thing keeping him grounded. His nervous habit. One thing that hasn't changed.

"Can I tell you something?"

"Sure," I say, standing up. "How about we go for a walk?"

We head around the side of the house, toward the trees. The air's colder here, the breeze sharper, slipping under my collar.

Lee walks in silence for a long minute.

"I didn't want to burden Lexy," he says at last. "She's so close to delivering, and I don't wanna dump all this on her. But I needed to talk to someone."

"I get it," I say. And I do.

He exhales, shaky. "It's the guilt. The anger. All of it just sits on my chest. I wake up already exhausted. Like I'm behind on a life I don't even remember living."

Something twists inside of me.

How does a person catch up to a life that was stolen from them?

"I get the anger part," I say quietly.

He stops walking. Rubs his head hard. I recognize that motion. I've done it myself when thoughts get too loud.

"I feel terrible, man."

He won't look at me. His voice thins, fraying at the edges.

"I remember that day. The day they took me. Pieces of it. But I don't remember Mom and Dad. I saw them in dreams growing up. But in my actual memory?" He shakes his head. "There's nothing."

He swallows hard.

"I remember you. I have one memory of Nicole. I remember how much I looked up to you, how I always wanted to hang out with you."

That almost breaks me. I never felt like someone worth looking up to back then.

His voice falters. "But the day they took me is the only

memory I have of our sister."

I glance at him. "What about me?"

He turns his head just slightly, like it costs him something to say this.

"I have one very vivid memory of you," he says. "You were teaching me how to ride a bike. I kept falling. Getting mad. Thinking I was the worst bike rider ever. You were beside me, coaching me through it... and then you fell too."

A faint, broken smile flickers.

"I remember being glad I wasn't the only one who fell."

His brow furrows, realization dawning slowly.

"You fell on purpose that day, didn't you?"

I let out a quiet chuckle, more breath than sound. "Yeah. I figured if you saw me eat dust too, you'd get back up."

Funny how one moment survived everything else.

"I remember our sword fights," Lee says with a small chuckle. He shakes his head, blinking fast. His eyes shine, like the grief has finally reached the surface.

I laugh along with him. Those were good times.

"That's all I have, man," he pleads. "That's all I can fucking remember."

His knees give out. He collapses to the ground, hands covering his face as a sob rips out of him—raw, unguarded, decades overdue.

"I feel so bad I don't remember Mom and Dad," he chokes. "They were my parents. How can I not remember them? They spent years crying over me. Searching for me. Thinking I was..."

He can't finish. The sobs take over. Years of weight pouring out in one breath.

I'm on my knees beside him before I think about it. My hand grips his shoulder, anchoring him.

The pain in his voice punches straight through me. I've spent years angry at the world for taking him. I never thought about how cruel it would be to give him back like this.

"We get it," I say, even as my own voice cracks. "We don't expect you to remember."

I bite down hard, but the tears still come.

"We're just glad you're..." My throat closes up. I force the word out. "Alive."

Tears fall freely now. No shame in them. I pull him into a hug, my arms tight around him like I can hold him steady through this hurricane of feelings we are drowning in. Thirty years of fear collapse into this one moment.

"It's okay you don't remember," I whisper. "We remember enough for all of us."

He pulls back slowly. I keep my hands on his shoulders, looking him straight in the eyes.

"My parents... our parents... they just want to get to know you, man. That's all. They have no expectations. It's gonna be awkward for all of us, but that feeling won't last forever."

He sniffs, wiping his face with his sleeve. He doesn't answer, but something shifts. The weight doesn't disappear; it redistributes.

I glance at my phone. I was supposed to call Anderson tonight. Talk through the Bevin Stanley case. Chase answers for another family.

I slide the phone back into my pocket.

It can wait.

The Stanley family deserves answers, but my brother deserves me.

"Hey," I say, nudging his shoulder the way I used to. "You wanna go somewhere with me tonight? Just the two of us?"

Lee looks at me. His eyes look tired but curious. "Where?"

"There are a couple of places I want to show you," I say. "They mean a lot to me."

He nods slowly. "Let me check with Lexy. If she's okay with me heading back later... I'm in."

"Sure thing," I reply.

As he texts, I watch him, memorizing this version of him. Not in fear of losing him again, but because I finally can.

CHAPTER 19

CALEB

The highway is quieter at night.

That's something I've always liked about it—the way the road stretches out like it's willing to listen to your sorrows. Lee sits in the passenger seat, hands folded in his lap, watching the white lines flick past us. He's been doing that the entire drive, like he's afraid to miss something important if he looks away. Or maybe he's afraid of my driving.

I keep the radio off. Tonight, silence says more than any song.

As we round a gentle curve, I ease onto the shoulder and kill the engine. The headlights spill over a battered guardrail and the scrub grass beyond. The metal whispers as it cools, and I feel its old familiarity settle around me.

This place still knows me.

"This is it," I say.

Lee turns slowly, uncertainty flickering in his eyes. "This…is what exactly?"

"This is where everything changed." The words land heavier than I expect, settling somewhere deep in my chest.

I step out, the night air cool and clean, and lean against the hood. Lee follows, standing beside me. For a moment we just listen to the wind moving through the trees. I let the quiet do some of the talking for me.

"I was on a date," I tell him. "Well, what was supposed to be a date."

He raises an eyebrow. "You weren't into it?"

I snort. "Yeah. My coworker Mark Conway set it up. Swore she was perfect for me. I wasn't really looking. We made small talk. No spark. No connection."

"Been there," he admits.

I point to a faint, oil-stained patch on the road. "I was driving home, already telling Mark it didn't work out." I motion a circle with my finger. "That is the spot I first saw Cassidy." I can still see it if I try hard enough.

Confusion crosses Lee's face.

"Barefoot. Dirty. Looked like she'd been walking for days." My throat tightens a little. "I stopped. Asked if she was okay. She couldn't even tell me her own name. No idea where she'd come from. Her eyes...they were blank, like someone had erased her past."

Lee's eyes stay on the road now, wide and fixed. I wonder what it's like for him, hearing someone else has lost important memories.

"I took her to the hospital. They ran tests, asked questions neither of us could answer. After the hospital, she had no place to go."

I trace a finger along the scratch in the hood. "So I brought her home. Put her in my guest room. Christ, Lee, I had no clue what I was doing."

Definitely didn't know I was opening the door to something that would change me forever.

Lee just stands there speechless.

"It was the strangest thing I've ever lived through," I admit, voice catching. "And also the most alive I've ever felt. I'd do it again in a heartbeat."

Lee exhales, the sound soft but certain. "Sounds like fate."

"Sounds like bad timing that turned into something good," I say. "Which is kind of our family specialty."

He shakes his head, a slow smile spreading. "That'll make one hell of a grandkid bedtime story," he laughs, unbelieving.

We get back in the truck and head farther out until the

pavement turns to gravel. The sound changes under the tires, familiar and comforting. We pull up at my cabin, and go inside.

I step inside, flip on the lights. Warm amber spills across the worn floorboards. "This is where we hid out," I tell him. Where the world stayed small enough to manage.

Lee moves through the room slowly, fingertips brushing the splintered tabletop, the scarred counter, the doorframe we once pressed our backs against. He's gathering proof of what we survived here.

We go out the back door, and I lead him down the path to the clearing.

"And this," I say, nodding toward the targets nailed into the wood, "is where I taught her how to shoot."

He blinks, his eyebrows rising a bit. "Cassidy?"

"She's a natural," I say, smiling. Still proud after all this time.

I hesitate. The moment stretches. Some truths don't like to be rushed.

"There's something else," I add.

He turns toward me.

"She killed a guy."

He laughs as if I told him a joke. "No way."

I keep my face still. "Little did I know at the time," I say quietly, "he was one of the boys with that woman who kidnapped you."

His eyes go wider. His mouth opens, then closes. "Are you serious?"

"Dead serious." I lean closer, dropping my voice. "And it gets even better. His brother abducted me, Cassidy, and my work partner. But that's a story for another night."

He runs a hand through his hair, pacing the length of the clearing once before stopping beneath the trees. "Wow."

An awkward hush falls, the night pressing in around us. I nod toward the cabin. "Let's go back inside."

Back in the living room, I crack open two cold beers and hand him one. Then I sink into the recliner next to the sofa. It feels strange and right all at once, sharing space like this.

He lifts his bottle, studies the amber liquid. "This," he says after a long pause, "is the guys' night I didn't know I was missing."

I clink my bottle against his. "The one we waited our whole lives for."

He takes a long swallow, then sets the bottle down with a soft thud. He starts testing memories like stones across water. "Remember when we built that rickety ramp in the backyard, and you tried to fly your bikes off it?"

I smile at the memory. He just remembered another thing.

"Yeah. I tore up my knee trying to show off, but pretended it didn't hurt because you were watching."

He grins. Then squints. "Did we go to Disneyland?"

The laugh comes easier this time. "Nope. Never happened. Must've been a dream."

His brow creases. "So I never puked on Goofy?"

I shake my head, warmth creeping into my voice. "Not with me. I'd remember something like that," I tell him, and we both burst out laughing.

Correcting his memories doesn't feel like a loss... it feels like proof that we're finally here, filling in the blanks together. Experiencing an evening of new memories those fuckers can never take from us.

CHAPTER 20

KARRIE

I used to tell myself silence was kindness, like a soft blanket draped over a wound so no one could see it bleeding.

I believed that keeping my mouth shut protected my family, protected me. Dredging up something from years ago wouldn't bring anyone back. It would only shatter the fragile normal we'd pieced together.

That was my story.

The truth was, I was terrified.

He wasn't just a teacher. He was my stepbrother. The responsible one. The one everyone trusted. My mom used to beam, pointing to him and my stepfather when she spoke of how lucky we were... how safe we finally felt.

The night Bevin went missing, I saw her get into Nick's car. I left that out for now. The detective has enough to start with.

Everyone remembers the rain. The search parties. Missing posters stuck to trees. What haunts me is that he never flinched when her name came up on the news. Not a single question. Just that tight mouth and those calm, practiced eyes.

I replayed that moment in my mind a hundred times, wondering if I'd imagined her stepping into his car. Maybe my grief had warped my vision. Maybe fear had painted in the blanks. I gulped down my doubts, convinced that—if I was wrong—speaking up would shatter our family over a baseless assumption.

Then, a few months ago, on the night of my mother's funeral, I found a copy of an email. I was sifting through old boxes in her study, when I spotted a folded letter tucked behind a trove of my stepfather's old things.

It was an email from a girl named Whitney, to my stepfather. In her email she called Nick, Mr. Bower. She said she felt uncomfortable with the teacher and didn't know who else to talk to. Admitting that my stepbrother made her feel uneasy.

In that instant, something inside me shifted. This was no longer a hazy, untrustworthy memory. It was a pattern.

My mom is gone now. The woman I stayed quiet for. The one who would've fallen apart if she'd known what I suspected.

I don't owe anyone silence anymore.

Nick's no longer my family.

So, I gave the detective the photo. The one I told myself meant nothing. The one that possibly means everything.

I didn't do it for justice or applause. I did it because I stopped caring about what happens to him. Because there are at least two girls he's preyed upon now.

Nick started asking me questions.

What time did I get home that night?

Was I with anyone else?

Where did I go that night?

I didn't understand what he was doing until he told the detectives he had been with me. He told them my exact night, entering himself into it, and said I would confirm his story.

Which I did.

But now it's time for the real truth to surface.

CHAPTER 21

CALEB

Our house sounds different when company is over.

Not louder, just fuller. Like the walls are finally doing the job they were built for. The hum of the refrigerator, the tick of the wall clock, even the soft scrape of chair legs on hardwood all feel alive.

Anderson is perched at the dining table, her charcoal blazer draped over the back of her chair. Cassidy is curled into the corner of the couch with her laptop balanced on her knees, and Nova is sprawled on the floor beside her with files spread out like she's mapping a crime scene on my rug.

I'm resting against the kitchen counter holding a cup of coffee, watching it all come together.

"Alright," Anderson says, rapping her silver pen against a yellow legal pad. "Let's talk about what we have so far for Bevin Stanley."

The name lodges in the air like a stone.

Cassidy's fingers freeze above the keyboard; the soft whirr of her laptop's fan is suddenly loud. Nova's head lifts, her expression sharpening. I know she's already sketching mental timelines and motives.

That's Nova for you. Always ten steps ahead.

"You go first," I quip.

Darcy flips one of the manila folders shut, the snap echoing. "I looked into this Nick Bower," she says, brushing a strand of hair behind her ear. "Ran a background check. Nothing major."

"That's not exactly reassuring," I reply, tracing the rim of my coffee mug with a fingertip.

She shrugs, gaze drifting to her laptop screen. "Mostly minor traffic violations. Speeding, a couple of careless-driving tickets. One DUI... about eleven years ago." She taps a key, and a line of text scrolls by. "Court-ordered rehab. Six months inpatient. Records show he completed it."

"I wonder if he stayed clean," I respond.

"As far as public records go," she answers, "there's nothing since."

I bring the mug to my lips and taste only bitterness. My coffee has gone cold. People treat spotless records like open windows into clean souls. Rarely does it work that way.

"Karrie was adamant that her stepbrother was involved," I say, glancing at Cass.

"It's possible," Anderson admits, leaning forward. "Whether he deserves it or not, he's in our lap now."

"We need to see what he's doing," I say. "The chief won't green-light an inquiry based on a photo from a cold case file."

Nova props herself up on one elbow, her eyes bright with challenge. "That's where we come in."

I shift, meeting Cassidy's expectant look. "So it's official?"

Cassidy's lips curve into a small, determined smile. "Yeah. We're starting a PI business."

"I'm partnering with her," Nova says. "Because she's good at details and I'm stubborn."

I smile despite myself. "You're both stubborn."

Cassidy's smile softens. There's something steady in her now. Purpose suits her.

Anderson clears her throat, straightening in her chair. "For what it's worth, it's the right move. You've got instincts that cops can't use. And far fewer rules. I've always said this was your calling."

Cassidy smiles. "I think so too."

The conversation flows on, half the meaning carried between glances and unspoken understanding. Minutes dissolve.

Eventually, Anderson rubs her face and exhales. "Okay, enough doom for one night."

I snort. "You were the one who invited the doom in."

"True," she concedes with a grin. "But I also bring gossip."

Cassidy perks up. "Oh?"

Anderson's smile turns mischievous. "I'm moving in with him."

I blink. "That was fast."

She shrugs, tilting her head. "When you know, you know."

Cassidy's eyes warm with happiness. "He seems good for you."

"He is," Anderson says, voice softer now. "Exactly what I needed."

I raise my mug in a playful toast. "I'm happy for you. After everything you've been through, you deserve someone solid."

She laughs off the seriousness, her shoulders relaxing as she shakes her head. "The office is still a mess, though."

"Shocker," I say dryly, plopping on the couch next to Cassidy.

"Mitchell's buried in paperwork up to his eyeballs. He took on too many projects, trying to outdo everyone as usual.

Merrick's still pretending he's not burned out, though the bags under his eyes tell a different story. Adams is... well... yeah. She is still Adams."

Cassidy laughs, a melodic sound that fills the room. "She's something alright."

Anderson's whole face changes. "Saw Mark's little guy the other day. He brought him by the office. He had on these tiny red sneakers that lit up when he walked."

"I bet he's getting big," I say, picturing a miniature version of Conway.

"He's so damn cute," Anderson replies, eyes crinkling at the corners. "Those chubby cheeks and that laugh... they sure make the cutest little family."

I smile, feeling a warmth spread through my chest, then clear my throat. "Speaking of family..."

Anderson's eyebrows shoot up, giving me a look that clearly says, "You knocked her up."

I roll my eyes, chuckling. "Don't go there. I took Lee out to the cabin the other night. Showed him some things."

Darcy's eyes warm like honey in sunlight. "How was it?"

"Good," I say, and mean it. "We talked. A lot. I think we bonded."

Anderson grins. "I'm glad to hear that."

It was one of the best nights of my life. Lee is so much more than I expected—thoughtful, quick-witted, with Mom's laugh and Dad's sense of humor. I guess I didn't know what to expect, since I only knew the kid version of him with scraped knees. He has turned into quite a good man.

Nova gathers the files, her silver rings catching the lamplight as she moves. "I'll dig deeper into Bower tomorrow. Rehab records sometimes hide more than they show."

"And I'll reach out to a few people he looks connected with," Cassidy adds. "See if his name rings bells outside the system."

Anderson stands, stretching. "Sounds like a plan. I'll see what else I can find with our resources without tipping the station off."

They make their way to the door, gathering their coats, saying goodbye, and the house returns to its stillness. Cassidy pauses at the door, slipping her warm hand into mine for a second, her fingers fitting between my own.

"You okay?" she asks, her eyes searching mine in the half-light.

I nod, feeling the truth seep into my body. "Yeah. I am."

For the first time in my life, I don't feel like something is missing. The hole in my soul is starting to fuse together.

Chapter 22

CALEB

The waiting room smells of lemon cleaner and old paper.

I sit in the same chair as last time, knees spread, hands locked together as if I let them go something worse will spill out. My fingers ache from how hard I'm gripping myself together. There's a framed print on the wall across from me, some kind of beach at sunrise.

That's new.

It's supposed to be calming. It just makes me think about time passing without my permission. About how the sun keeps rising whether you're ready to face the day or not.

It's my second session today.

The first one was pretty rough. It left me feeling really exposed.

Last time we talked about Lee. About what it felt like to see my brother walk back into my life after thirty years of not knowing if he was dead or buried under a different name. I'd thought that was the big thing. The thing therapy was for.

Turns out it was just the door.

"Mr. Reed?" the receptionist says.

I stand, my knees stiff, my throat already tight like it knows what's coming, and follow her down the hallway. It's the same office. Same couch. Same chair angled just enough that you don't feel interrogated but still feel seen.

Dr. Wagman smiles at me, calm and patient in a way that makes me want to grit my teeth. "Good to see you again."

I nod. "Yeah."

I sit. The silence stretches, waiting to be filled. My chest feels heavy, like there's a weight pressing down from the inside.

"You brought something up at the end of the last session. Do you still want to talk about that today?" she inquires.

The carpet has a tiny dark stain near my shoe. I focus on it because if I look up, I might not be able to speak.

"I do."

"What happened?"

I let out a breath that feels like it's been stuck in my lungs for weeks. "I was abducted."

She doesn't flinch. Just nods slightly, inviting me to keep

going.

"Me, my fiancée Cassidy, and my work partner, Detective Merrick," I say. "We were taken because Cassidy killed a man in self-defense. He was trying to kill her. He'd already kidnapped her once before that, stripped her memory."

My jaw tightens. I can feel the muscles in my face starting to hurt, like I'm holding something back physically.

"They tied us up. Put them in chairs, and I was tied to a pole in the center of the room."

I swallow hard. It feels like trying to force sand down my throat.

"He made me choose who would live."

Dr. Wagman leans forward just a little. Her eyes widen before she can stop it.

"Caleb," she says carefully, "I want you to pause for a second. Notice where that sentence landed in your body."

I laugh weakly. "Everywhere."

She nods. "That makes sense."

She taps her pen on her notepad. "Who made you choose?"

"The man who took us. The brother of the guy Cassidy killed." I laugh without humor.

I rub my hands over my face. "He lined them up. Cassidy on one side. Merrick on the other."

My chest tightens like it does every time I think about it.

"I chose Cassidy."

The words land heavy in the room.

The therapist doesn't rush in. She lets the silence do its thing.

Dr. Wagman exhales slowly. "You were placed in an impossible moral position," she says. "Your nervous system was hijacked. This wasn't logic. It was survival."

"I didn't even hesitate," I continue, anger creeping into my voice. "That's the part that eats at me. I didn't think. I just... chose her."

My throat burns. It feels raw, like I've been screaming for hours even though I haven't raised my voice.

I squeeze my eyes shut. "Merrick didn't argue. Didn't plead. He just looked at me and nodded as if he understood."

My hands are shaking now. I press them together harder, but it doesn't help.

"The guy squeezed the trigger," I say. "Aimed right at Merrick's head."

Dr. Wagman inhales sharply. She doesn't hide it this time.

I suck in a breath, taking a moment to steady myself. A tear slips out anyway, hot and sudden, tracking down my cheek before I can stop it. I don't wipe it away.

"The gun misfired."

I open my eyes, staring at nothing. "And for half a second I thought… I thought that was it. That I got him killed." My voice cracks despite my best efforts. My throat tightens until it actually hurts. "The guy raised the gun to shoot again."

"And then?" she asks softly.

"And then we were saved. I don't even remember all of it." I shake my head. It feels so heavy, as if my neck can barely hold it up. "But that moment is burned into my head."

I lean back, anger surging through me again. "I can't look Merrick in the face. He says he's fine. But how the hell could he be? I almost got the guy killed."

Dr. Wagman watches me carefully. Her expression is no longer neutral. It's shaken.

She is quiet for a long moment. "Survivor's guilt," she says finally. "Moral injury. Those are symptoms."

"He didn't die, though. So how can I have survivor's guilt?"

"Someone doesn't have to die for that emotion to come. Someone can be close to death because of you, and that can set it off," she clarifies.

"Why did you choose Cassidy?" she asks.

The question hits harder than I expect.

"Because I love her," I say immediately. "Because she'd

already been through hell. She was already a victim in all of it."

"And Merrick?"

"He's my friend," I snap. Then quieter, ashamed of the snap, "He's my partner."

"Do you believe you wanted Merrick dead?" she asks.

"No," I say fiercely. My voice comes out louder than I mean it to. "Never."

"Do you believe Cassidy deserved to die?"

"No."

She nods. "So you were forced into an impossible choice under threat of violence."

"That doesn't make it better," I say. "It just makes me a coward with a reason."

"It makes you human under duress," she corrects.

She studies me for a moment. Really studies me.

"Let me ask you something different."

I sigh. "Alright."

"If Merrick had been the one forced to choose," she says, "and the choice was between you and the woman he loves, what would you expect him to do?"

An image springs into my mind. Merrick chained to a pole. The perps gun pointed at me. A woman Merrick cares for in a chair next to me.

My chest tightens again, but this time it's different.

"I'd want him to choose her," I admit.

She nods. "That answer came fast."

The realization lands like a punch to the ribs.

"Why?" she asks.

"Because that's his person," I say slowly. "Because if he didn't, he'd never forgive himself. Because protecting your woman is what we do as men."

"And would you hold that choice against him?" she asks.

I shake my head. "No."

"Would you think he was weak?"

"No," I say again, more firmly. "I'd think he was doing exactly what he was supposed to do."

She lets that sit between us.

"You're a cop," she says. "What do you believe your job is, at its core?"

I swallow. My throat still aches. "To protect people. To risk it all if I have to."

"Even yourself?" she asks.

"Yes."

She nods. "That includes emotional risk. Impossible decisions. You didn't fail Merrick, Caleb. You acted out of love, not malice. And the responsibility for that gun is not yours."

I look down at my hands. They're still shaking, but less. Like the storm hasn't passed, but the wind has slowed.

"I still hate myself for it," I admit.

"That doesn't make you wrong," she says. "It makes you human."

She glances at the clock. "Before we end today, I want to give you something to work on."

I look up. "Okay."

"This week," she says, "I want you to write two letters. You don't have to give them to anyone."

I tense up.

"One to Merrick. Say everything you're afraid to say to his face. The anger, the guilt, the fear."

I nod slowly.

"The second letter," she continues, "is to yourself. From Merrick. Write what you believe he would say to you if he knew everything you're carrying."

"Okay. I think I can do that," I say.

I'm not sure how that will help me, but I need to try something.

The session ends too soon. Or maybe just in time.

"We're out of time for today," she says gently. "I know this was heavy work."

I nod, even though my head still feels foggy. Like I'm standing at the edge of something and didn't realize how far down it went.

"I want you to be mindful of how your body feels when you leave here," she adds. "Drink water. Ground yourself. Therapy has a way of making a person feel unsettled and unbalanced for a period of time after."

I let out a slow breath. "Okay."

She stands, and I follow, my legs stiff but steady. The room feels different now. Less like a trap. More like a place I survived.

At the door, she pauses. "We'll keep working on this," she says. "You don't have to carry it all at once."

She opens the door and gestures for me to step into the hallway. The movement feels symbolic somehow.

At the front desk, she turns to the receptionist. "Let's get Mr. Reed scheduled for next week. Same time, if possible."

The receptionist taps on the keyboard. "Thursday at four?"

I hesitate for half a second, then nod. "That works."

Dr. Wagman looks back at me. "Between now and then," she says, "focus on the letters. And if it feels overwhelming, stop. This isn't about forcing anything."

"Alright," I say quietly.

She offers a small, reassuring smile. "You did good work today."

Her words catch me off guard.

"Thanks," I manage.

When I step outside, the air feels a little lighter. For the first time, I think maybe Merrick isn't lying when he says he's okay. And maybe one day I will be too.

CHAPTER 23

CALEB

When I get home, Cassidy is hunched over the kitchen island with her open laptop, fingers paused above the keyboard as if she's just struck digital gold. Her golden hair falls in a curtain around her face, and there's that unmistakable spark in her eyes... the look of someone who's pieced together a puzzle.

I slip my keys onto the iron hook by the door, then cross behind her. My arms slide around her waist, drawing her close, and I press a quick kiss to her cheek. The warmth of her skin against mine feels like home. "Find something?" I murmur.

She tilts her head back, with that same bright intensity in her gaze. "Yeah. We found where Nick's staying."

That gets my attention. My heart hops. I pivot, pressing my hip against the cool marble of the counter, and lean in. "Where?"

Cassidy taps a few keys, the screen shifting to a grainy satellite image. "Small rental on the edge of town. Kind of run-down. One neighbor close enough to see him come and go." She pauses, watching my face. "I talked to the neighbor."

"And?" I prompt, every nerve suddenly alert.

She glances at me, gauging my expression. "He said the only odd thing he's noticed about my brother..." She trails off.

"Brother?" I cut in, lifting my brows.

Her lips curve into a slow, deliberate smile. "Yes. My brother."

I shake my head, a chuckle escaping me. "Good one."

She beams, satisfied. "Anyway, he says that Nick keeps a very specific schedule."

I fold my arms, leaning forward. "Go on."

Cassidy's fingers drum the countertop as she recounts. "He leaves at five in the morning. Like clockwork. Gets home around five in the evening. Then leaves again at six-thirty. Comes back. Leaves again at ten." She exhales. "Sometimes even at two in the morning."

I frown. "Every day?"

"Pretty much. The neighbor swears it's always those times."

"That's... odd." I rub my jaw. My years as a cop ignite behind my eyes, scanning for patterns, motives. "Too regimented."

"Exactly," Cassidy agrees. "Nova thinks he's meeting someone."

"Could be," I say, pushing off the counter and pacing a slow arc across the floor. The wooden planks creak under my steps. "So, what's the plan?"

She snaps the laptop closed with a decisive click. "Nova and I will follow him. Find out who he's seeing, what he's up to."

The hell you are, I think to myself.

I halt mid-stride, narrowing my eyes at her. "Absolutely not."

Cassidy arches a brow. Her voice is calm but firm as she sets her hands on her hips. "Babe..."

"I should go with you," I insist. "If you're tailing someone, you need backup."

She moves closer, grips my forearms gently. "No. I don't want you risking your badge on a private tail. Especially with everything else you've got going on."

I open my mouth to argue, but her logic lands like a lead weight. Swallowing my frustration, I mutter, "Fine."

Then I turn away, dragging my hand through my hair, and head to the cabinet. I pour a shot of whiskey into a crystal tumbler, the amber liquid swirling before I drink it in one burning gulp. I welcome the fire slithering down my throat.

From the fridge I grab a beer, the hiss of carbonation punctuating the tense silence, as it pops open. Leaning back against the counter, I let the cold brew cool the burn.

Cassidy watches me, concern rippling over her features where confidence just moments ago stood firm. "You've been drinking more lately," she says softly.

I stiffen, clenching my teeth. "I'm fine."

She cranks her head. "I didn't say you weren't."

"It feels like you did," I respond, opening my eyes big. I can't believe I have to defend myself right now.

There's a beat of silence.

"Well, then... what's your point, Cass?" I snap, immediately regretting the sharpness of my tone.

She scoffs in defense. "I'm sorry," she says quietly. "For caring."

Ouch! She got me there.

My shoulders sag, and I let out a slow breath. "No. That's not what I meant." I rub my face with one hand, the tension in my muscles screaming. "I'm just... on edge."

She steps closer, resting a hand on my arm. "I know."

I take a sip of the beer, slower this time, feeling the carbonation from the beer prickling at the back of my mouth.

"Therapy's stirring stuff up. The Lee thing. Merrick. It's a bit much to process."

I don't tell her about the shame that floods me whenever our eyes meet. Something about her bothers me now, something that wasn't there before. It's like a hidden bruise that aches whenever the skin is touched; the feeling of shame and confusion hovers just below the surface, a constant companion that I can't quite make sense of.

My throat tightens, constricting around the words. "It feels like every time I start to breathe, something else comes up."

Cassidy's thumb traces a small circle against my sleeve. "You don't have to be okay all at once."

I huff a weak laugh that feels hollow in my chest. "I kind of feel like I do."

She looks up at me, keeping her eyes steady. "You don't."

I meet her gaze, something in my chest loosening like a knot being untied.

"You're not broken," she adds softly. "You're healing. And yeah, it's messy. But you're still here. That counts."

I nod, the defensive edge fading like mist. "I'm sorry I snapped."

She smiles faintly, just a slight upturn at the corners of her mouth. "Apology accepted."

I take another sip, then set the beer down on the counter with a soft clink. "Just... be careful with Nick. Promise me."

"I promise," she says, her fingers squeezing my arm once.

I pull her into a hug, her hair smelling faintly of berries, holding on a second longer than usual. Her shoulders drop as she exhales, her fingers loosening their grip on my sleeve.

Letting her go, I step back, feeling the weight of her words sink into my skin.

CHAPTER 24

CASSIDY

Nick Bower leaves at 10:00 PM.

Not around then. Not give or take a few minutes. Exactly. Just like the neighbor said. I glance at the dash clock, then back up at the building across the street, like maybe tonight will be different. It isn't. The door opens on cue, and Nick Bower steps out into the thin yellow glow of the entry light like he's hitting a mark onstage.

Nova shifts beside me in the passenger seat, slow and careful, like she's afraid even movement might tip him off. We're both dressed in black to blend in with the night.

Nick locks the door behind him. One turn of the key. He doesn't look over his shoulder. Doesn't scan the lot. Doesn't act like a man who's been carrying a secret for years.

That's the first thing that nags at me.

He stands there for a second, pulling his phone from his

pocket. The screen lights his face, and I watch him read something—really read it, not just glance. His thumb hovers, then taps once. He slips the phone away like whatever just happened is done now.

Permission given.

Nova exhales quietly. "There he goes."

Nick starts walking, cutting left instead of heading straight toward the main road. Same as last night and the night before. He avoids the well-lit streets.

I lift my camera and zoom in. When he passes under the streetlight at the corner, I get a clear view of his face. The shutter clicks softly. I take two more, my finger steady even though my pulse jumps.

We wait another five minutes, just in case he were to circle back. He doesn't. When the street settles again, we move.

We don't go for the door. Too obvious. Too risky.

Nova leads us around the side of the building, where the concrete narrows and the light dies completely. No windows facing us. No neighboring buildings close enough to see. The most secluded part of the place.

She whispers, "This is a bad idea."

"I know," I whisper back.

"This is a really bad idea."

"Yep."

"Just checking that we agree this is insane."

I give her a look in the dark. "You ready or not?"

She sighs. "I hate that you say that like there's an option."

The window slides open easier than it should. That bothers me more than if it had fought back. Nova holds it steady while I climb in, careful not to scrape the sill. My boots hit the floor without a sound. The smell of cinnamon hits my nose immediately.

Nova slips in behind me, easing the window shut.

The place feels unreal. The knowledge that someone could be dangerous, maybe worse than anything I've imagined, makes every heartbeat echo in my ears.

No signs of violence.

Whatever that would look like.

The air feels watched. I catch myself holding my breath, like the place might notice us if I don't.

We don't touch more than we have to. Nova checks the kitchen. I head to the bedroom. Along the way, I notice small things that don't line up—a calendar on the wall with every day blank except one circled date that repeats each month.

The dresser drawers are neat to the point of being suspicious.

The closet is worse. It looks like someone copied a checklist of what a man should own and stopped there.

It's the nightstand that does it.

I slide the drawer open and stop.

IDs. Three of them. Different names. Different states.

Being inside a possible murderer's space... the knowledge that someone could have taken lives here, hits me differently than any crime show I've ever seen. My stomach tightens as I spread them out carefully.

Nick Bower. Tyler Knell. Kevin McLean.

"That's not normal," I whisper to myself. "Why does this guy have so many identities?"

"Cass," Nova says from the other room, low and sharp.

I join her in the kitchen. She's holding a phone. Not his everyday one, but a cheap burner that was tucked behind the microwave.

"No lock on it. It looks like only one contact," she says. "And just one call a week."

I take a picture of the number with my phone. It looks like a Seattle number.

This is so weird.

I think about the neighbor, so confident in his observations. Think about the routine, the timing, the way he checked his phone before leaving like someone else was keeping the clock.

Nova reaches up toward the top of the cabinets, fingertips brushing something she didn't see. A small ceramic figurine wobbles and falls to the ground.

"Oh, shit!" Nova shouts.

It doesn't shatter, but we both freeze, staring at it as if it might make noise on its own.

Nova gently sets it back exactly where it was, hands shaking just enough to notice. "Okay," she whispers. "That's our signal to leave."

"Yeah," I agree. "Before something actually breaks."

We put everything back exactly how we found it, slipping out the window again. By the time we're back in the car, my hands are shaking like I have Parkinson's.

I pull the camera out again and scroll through the photos. The streetlight shot is perfect.

I dial Caleb before I can second-guess myself.

He answers right away. "You got something?"

"Yeah," I say, staring at the frozen image of the man.

I send the photos through.

The one of his face. The picture of the IDs.

There's a pause on the line. Long enough.

"That's not him," Caleb finally says.

"Really?" I ask.

"I've studied his picture. That is not Karrie's stepbrother. I know it. I can ask her just to make sure." He exhales sharply. "How did you get photos of IDs, Cass?"

I hesitate exactly half a second. "We broke in."

"You... what?" His voice jumps an octave. "Cassidy, you cannot just... Jesus."

"It's done," I cut in. "There's no point arguing."

Silence. Then, quieter, "You two need to get out of there."

I lean back against the headrest and look out at the quiet street. "So, we've got the wrong guy?" I question.

"Looks like it. By the IDs, I doubt Nick is his real name. You two need to get out of there."

Headlights sweep across the building.

Nova stiffens. "Cass."

His truck pulls up.

Thirty minutes early.

"Oh no," I whisper. "Did he know we were in there?"

Nova meets my eyes, fear sharp and alive between us. "Let's go."

We pull away from the curb without headlights, rolling silently until we hit the corner and finally breathe again. I glance at my phone, the Seattle number burned into my camera roll, and itching my curiosity.

CHAPTER 25

KARRIE

The room smells like three-dollar Merlot and artificially buttered popcorn, the kind of accidental pairing that only happens when I've abandoned all pretense of adulthood for the night. My favorite glass lamp, filled with a base full of seashells, perches on the side table, spilling a lazy pool of amber light across the living-room rug, leaving the corners to brood in shadow. The weight of my overheating laptop burns through my fleece pajama pants as some bearded comedian with pit stains jokes about TSA pat-downs.

My phone lights up on the coffee table, illuminating a ring-shaped water stain on the wood.

Who would be calling at 11:37 PM?

That is the dead zone between late night and midnight, when even the most persistent spam callers have surrendered to silence.

I glance at the name. *The other reason Corey is dead.*

I forgot I had saved Detective Reed into my phone like that. God, I really need to update his contact info before someone glimpses it over my shoulder.

I swipe, pressing the glass against my ear. "Hello?" My voice comes out slurred.

"Is this Karrie?" His tone is steady, deliberate, the way people sound when they're trained not to reveal anything accidentally. Every syllable feels weighted.

I set my drink aside. "Yes," I swallow a knot of dread. "Hey."

"Good. I'm sending you something."

My phone vibrates against my cheek before I can ask what. A photo loads in, sharp and clear. A man under a streetlight, face caught mid-step.

"Is this Nick?" Caleb's voice drops to that quiet, measured tone detectives use, as if he already knows the answer.

I hunch forward, elbows digging into my thighs, squinting at the screen until my eyes water. The streetlamp reflects off damp hair, carving his face into light and shadow.

"That's not him."

I hear Reed's slow exhale, sounding as if air is escaping a punctured tire. "I didn't think so."

Frowning, I pinch the image and zoom deeper, as if squinting harder might provoke recognition. His features tease me, perched on the edge of memory. A name hovers just out of reach, like a word lodged behind my teeth.

A hush stretches between us, then I say, "But... I've seen that guy before."

On the other end, Caleb goes silent. I can almost hear his detective mind clicking into gear. "You have?"

"Yeah." I frown, creasing my forehead as I chase the memory. My thoughts shuffle through half-forgotten scenes like a deck of faded photographs. "I think he's one of Nick's friends."

"Do you know his name?"

"No," I admit, the frustration knotting in my stomach. These missing details jab at me like splinters; the harder I tug, the deeper they go. "I don't."

Caleb exhales, shifting tactics. "Cassidy found a number tied to this guy. Seattle area code." He rattles off the digits, each one clipped and precise.

I snatch a pen from the coffee table and scribble the numbers across an unopened bill. The paper crinkles under my grip. "Doesn't ring a bell."

"I tried calling it," he says. "No answer. Do you by chance

know where Nick lives now?"

A humorless bark escapes me. "No. I haven't seen him in over a year."

"Do you think he's in Spokane?"

"No." The word flies out too quickly, too certain for something I can't explain. "I don't think so."

Another pause. Heavier one this time. The kind that moves pieces around the board without either of us touching them.

Caleb's voice finally emerges, a single word that carries the weight of surrender. "Okay."

We don't say goodbye. We just hang up, both knowing something fundamental has shifted between us.

I stare at the photo again. My reflection stares back at me faintly from the screen.

My thumb hovers over the Seattle number. This is a bad idea, a voice whispers in my head. I press down anyway before my brain can catch up.

Someone answers.

"Hello?" a soft voice greets me.

It's a woman.

My heart hammers so hard it steals my breath. Heat blooms in my cheeks; cold sweat prickles under my arms. For a fraction of a second, I forget why I called at all.

"Hi," I force out, my voice steadier than I feel. "Is Nick there?"

The pause stretches like taffy, sticky and uncomfortable.

"Wrong number," she replies. The line clicks dead.

The words hit me like a freight train, thrusting me back to Aunt Judy's cluttered backyard. I can smell charcoal and sunscreen mingling in the July air. Bevin and I set up the cornhole boards while the other kids shrieked through sprinklers nearby.

Then her phone rang.

"Some kid in my class had the wrong number," she'd said with that half-smile, sliding the phone into the pocket of her cutoff shorts.

My own screen flicks to black in my hand. My lungs feel packed with concrete. That voice may be older, but it's undeniably hers.

That was Bevin.

CHAPTER 26

CALEB

TWO DAYS LATER

The rain is relentless, hammering the roof of the car like thousands of impatient fingertips, smearing the city lights into watercolor streaks across the windshield. I keep one hand on the wheel, the other drumming nervously against my thigh. My fingers are stiff from gripping too tightly, and I keep flexing them to shake out the tension. Cassidy is sitting beside me, calm as ever, watching the road. She doesn't need to say anything. Just having her here makes the knot in my chest loosen its stranglehold.

Red taillights drift in and out of focus ahead, glowing like distant embers through the rain. Now and then a semi roars past in the opposite lane, spraying sheets of water across the windshield that leave me half blind for a few seconds. Dark shapes of trees blur together along the roadside, broken only by the occasional gas station.

Nova and Karrie occupy the backseat like opposing weather systems. Nova's propped up against the door, combat boots crossed at the ankles, her vintage leather camera bag tucked protectively under her arm like a sleeping pet. The metal buckle clinking softly every time we hit a bump. She keeps making little comments, just loud enough for everyone to hear.

Karrie perches on the edge of her seat, chewing on her nail, while her other hand is clutching her phone. She glances at me every few seconds, her wide eyes reflecting the passing streetlights as if she's counting down to some inevitable catastrophe.

"Seattle," I mutter, shaking my head as raindrops race each other down the side window. "I can't believe we're actually doing this."

Cassidy glances at me, her expression steady as a lighthouse. "We have to. If what Karrie says is true... we can't ignore it."

Karrie leans forward, the scent of her vanilla perfume briefly cutting through Cassidy's car. "I swear it was her. I'd never forget her voice." She twists a strand of her hair nervously.

Nova snorts. "Are you sure it's not just wishful thinking?"

"I'm sure," Karrie snaps. She looks down at her phone, biting her lip. "It's her. I know it."

Silence settles over the car after that, thick and uncomfortable. The only sounds are the rain, the wipers, and the low hum of tires gliding over wet asphalt.

I catch Cassidy's eyes with a look, then refocus on the rain-slicked highway where headlights blur into golden smears. "I can't believe she's alive. After all these years."

Cassidy reaches over, her fingers brushing my forearm where I've rolled up my flannel sleeve. Her hand is warm and steady, grounding me in a way nothing else can, bringing me back to a memory of this case.

I was standing in the middle of the cereal aisle, staring blankly at a wall of colorful boxes. It had been a couple of months since Bevin disappeared, and her face was still everywhere.

Bevin's dad rounded the corner with a shopping cart that squeaked with every rotation of the wheel. He looked thinner than I remembered in that moment; his clothes were hanging off him as if they belonged to someone else.

"Detective," he said, surprised.

I asked him how he was holding up, because that's what you say in situations like that. Empty words everyone uses when there's nothing else left.

He shrugged in a stiff way. "Kids run off," he muttered. "They think they know better."

His words hit wrong.

He didn't seem worried, or even grieving for that matter. Just... annoyed. Like she inconvenienced him.

I remember telling myself people handle grief differently. That there's no right way to react when your daughter disappears. But something about the way he said it ate at me.

Then he said, quieter, "Sometimes they bring things on themselves."

I waited for him to explain what that meant, but he just gave me this thin smile, like he had already said too much.

I stood there long after he walked away; the squeak of that cart echoing down the aisle gave me a cold feeling in my gut. Something was off. I felt it then, and I still feel it now. But a feeling isn't proof. And I never had proof.

Then there was the journal thing.

Her parents gave it to me a week after she disappeared. One entry talked about an argument. A physical altercation she had with someone and how she would never forgive him. The next page was ripped out. I remember running my finger along the edge, knowing that was the page where she wrote who it was.

Who hurt her.

Who she was afraid of.

I asked her parents about it. They said they'd never seen that page. Said maybe Bevin tore it out herself.

Maybe she did.

Or maybe they are hiding something.

I tighten my grip on the steering wheel without realizing it. The tires hiss against the wet pavement, pulling me back to the present, but the unease lingers like a bruise pressed too hard.

If she really is alive... maybe I'll finally get the answers that have been clawing at the inside of my mind for years.

CHAPTER 27

KARRIE

The car rolls to a stop a block from the house. I can feel my hands shaking before I even step out. Rain ticks steadily against the windshield, softer now than before, but constant. My chest is pounding like it's trying to escape my ribcage.

"Let me go first," I say. "She knows me best."

"I think we should both go. Cassidy and Nova should wait in the vehicle," Caleb responds, his jaw set in that stubborn way that creates a tiny dimple in his left cheek.

"I don't know if that's a good..." I retort.

He interrupts with, "It's happening. You are not going to that door alone."

I scoff as I wrench open the car door. Cool, damp air hits my face as I step outside. Somewhere nearby, water is dripping steadily from a gutter. I see a truck turn right at the end of the otherwise dead street.

Each sound sends electric jolts through my already frayed nerves.

The house looks smaller than I expected. Just another place on a quiet street. Nothing about it looks special. Nothing about it looks like the place where everything might finally make sense.

For a second, I just stand there staring at the faded red door. Then, I knock. Nothing. I knock again, my knuckles stinging against the wood. I hear shuffling footsteps inside.

The door swings open. A boy, maybe nineteen, appears on the other side. He squints at us through sleepy eyes. He is wearing a faded, wrinkled t-shirt, looking as if he'd just woken up.

"Uh... can I help you?" he says, one hand still gripping the edge of the door.

I swallow, trying to sound calm, though my voice shakes. "Is Nick here?"

His expression flickers... confused, suspicious, maybe even a little scared. The corner of his mouth twitches. "Who...?"

Before I can answer, a soft voice calls from behind him: "Who is it?"

It's faint, hesitant, but I know it. That gentle lilt at the end of the sentence. My heart thuds so loudly I'm sure they all can hear it.

I push my hand against the doorframe. "Bevin!" I yell, my voice cracking with desperation.

The boy's eyes widen in alarm as he throws his weight against the door. I wedge my shoulder into the gap and shove back with everything I have. "Bevin! It's Karrie!"

The door flies open, crashing against the faded mint green wallpaper inside with a thunderous bang that echoes through the cramped entryway. The teen stumbles back a step, startled, his hands half raised like he doesn't know whether to push me or run.

A woman with deep shadows under her eyes rounds the corner. Her oversized flannel shirt hangs off one shoulder, revealing a faded tattoo.

"There's no Bevin here," she says firmly, crossing her arms over her chest.

I glare at her, taking in the nervous twitch of her eyebrow. "Is Nick here?" My voice wavers despite my clenched jaw.

She shakes her head, a strand of loose hair falling across her face. "No."

Then I see her. Bevin steps around the corner, and her hazel eyes lock onto mine. My heart stutters to a halt. She stares, frozen, her chapped lips parting slightly. Her face is gaunt, with new lines etched around her mouth, but unmistakably hers. Her hair, once flowing past her shoulders, is now cropped just below her ears and dyed an auburn color instead of her natural honey blonde. But the tiny scar on the side of her nose gives her away. It's her. It's really her.

For a second, no one breathes. The ceiling fan above us creaks with each rotation.

Bevin steps forward, trying to fill the silence. "I'm Bridget," she says quickly.

Something clicks in my head. My stomach plummets to my feet. Bevin isn't answering to her real name. She's hiding behind this fabricated identity, and these two may not even know the woman they're living with.

I breathe out slowly, trying to keep from passing out. My thoughts collide and scatter like startled birds.

She's alive.

CHAPTER 28

KARRIE

Bevin hesitates for a moment, then steps back, motioning for me to follow with slender fingers that tremble slightly. "Come upstairs," she mumbles. Her voice carries a strange mix of fear and relief, like she's letting me in on a dangerous secret.

I glance back over my shoulder at Caleb. He looks just as stunned as I feel, like he's afraid if he blinks she'll vanish again.

"Wait," I say, turning back to Bevin. "Can my friend come too?" My heart pounds against my ribs as I pray she doesn't recognize him as the detective who spent months dissecting her disappearance.

She hesitates for a second, her eyes flicking past me toward Caleb. Her shoulders tense slightly, as if she's bracing for someone to overhear. I can practically see the calculations happening in her mind.

For a moment, I think she's going to say no.

Then she nods, a quick, jerky movement. "Okay," she replies.

Relief washes over me so fast my knees feel weak.

Bevin leads us up a narrow staircase, the ancient wood groaning and creaking under our feet like it's telling secrets of its own. The steps dip slightly in the middle from years of use. I watch her feet as she climbs. She's wearing mismatched socks: one black, one dark blue with a hole at the heel. Her hand trails along the wall as she walks.

The hallway upstairs is dim. The air smells of lavender laundry detergent and old oak, the kind of scent that seeps into your clothes and stays there. It feels lived in. Normal. Terrifyingly normal for someone who's been missing for years.

She leads us into a small room at the end of the hall. The walls are a pale buttercup yellow, decorated with posters, but there's a warmth here that wasn't in my imagination all these years. A neatly made bed sits against one wall, with a folded sweater resting on the corner. A chipped blue ceramic mug with a hairline crack running down its side sits on the nightstand beside a dog-eared paperback lying face down, its spine permanently creased. I glance at the title... *The Last Thread* by Michelle Powers. Fitting, I think. This might be the last thread left to solving this case.

She closes the door behind us. The soft click of the latch catching makes my stomach tighten like a fist. It feels strange being shut in a room with someone who was supposed to be gone forever.

Caleb stays near the door, as if he's not sure he's allowed to come any farther. His eyes don't leave her face, tracking every expression like memorizing a map.

"I… I want to tell you," she begins, her voice barely above a whisper. "About what happened before… and how he saved me."

I already know it's going to be awful, but I can't look away. Part of me wants to interrupt, to ask a thousand questions all at once, but the words stay stuck in my throat.

Bevin takes a deep breath that makes her thin shoulders rise and fall, as if she's preparing herself to go back in time. "My mother hated me. My dad… he…" Her voice cracks, and she swallows hard. "It was bad. Really bad. I didn't have siblings to protect me. I was alone. No one saw what happened when the doors closed."

I nod gently, trying to encourage her, though my neck feels stiff as rusted metal. Out of the corner of my eye, I see Caleb's hands curl into fists.

"And then... Mr. Bower came into my life. He gave me a way out. A way to disappear. They couldn't find me, and eventually they stopped looking. I was finally safe." Her hands twist nervously in her lap. "I've been living as Bridget Monroe ever since. That's who I am now. I want to keep it that way."

Her eyes flick toward the hallway, toward the murmur of voices from the other people in the house. Her gaze lingers on the door like she expects it to open at any second. I was right. None of them know each other's real names. Each one has protection, a layer of safety, and Nick is the only one carrying the truth.

I take a shaky breath that doesn't quite fill my lungs. Caleb shifts slightly behind me, and I can practically feel the storm of thoughts running through his head.

The sound of footsteps interrupts us.

All three of us freeze.

The door opens with a prolonged creak, and Nick steps in, his six-foot frame filling the doorway. His eyes are sharp and calculating, and his gaze lands on Bevin first. Then they snap to me. Then Caleb.

"Bridget," he says firmly, his voice filling the small room like suffocating smoke. "What are you doing?"

His eyes narrow on us, pupils contracting to pinpoints, and

I feel the weight of that glare like it's trying to pin me to the floor. It's the kind of look that makes it clear he's used to being in control, to having his orders followed without question. A look I have seen far too many times across the dinner table, while he was lying to our parents.

Bevin stays seated, her hands tightening in her lap. "I'm talking to Karrie," she replies.

Nick's stare shifts fully to Caleb now, and the air in the room gets thicker, charged with tension. Harder to breathe in, like at a higher altitude. His jaw flexes once, as if he's biting back whatever he wants to say first.

"Karrie," he says in a frustrated tone that scrapes like sandpaper, "you need to leave."

No one moves. My legs feel rooted to the floor. The ticking of a distant clock counts the seconds of our standoff.

Bevin swallows hard, the sound audible in the silence, looking between us with a small, pleading expression that crinkles the corners of her eyes. "It's okay," she whispers, her breath catching. "They need to hear this."

I look at the floor, trying to calm my nerves. My pulse throbs in my fingertips. Caleb steps a little farther into the room, like he's committing to being here now, no matter what happens next. Close enough that we're all standing in the same small space, with no easy way out if things go wrong.

This is it.

The story we've been chasing for years sits right in front of us. And somehow, now that we're here, it feels bigger than I ever imagined.

CHAPTER 29

CALEB

I glance at Karrie, then back at Bevin and Nick. "I need to understand," I say, my voice cracking slightly. "All of it. What happened... and why?"

Bevin and Nick exchange a look—quick but loaded with unspoken history. The kind that says they've rehearsed this conversation a hundred times. Finally, Bevin nods, her chin dipping just once.

Her voice is steady at first, but her hands twist together in her lap as if she's trying to hold herself together. I stay quiet, letting her talk, afraid that even breathing too loudly might make her stop.

"My mom hated me. No idea why. They never planned to have me, so that may be part of it." She draws in a gasp of air. "And my dad, he didn't stop her abuse. Sometimes he..." She trails off, shaking her head, her hair falling across one eye.

"Sometimes he made it worse."

My jaw tightens until I feel my molars grind together.

"It wasn't just yelling," she continues, her eyes fixed on a stain on the ceiling. "It was hitting. Getting thrown into things. I had bruises a lot." She gives a small, hollow laugh. "I got good at hiding them. Hoodies. Long sleeves. Even in summer."

Images flash through my head before I can stop them. Bevin with a split lip, claiming she walked into a door. Bevin with purple fingerprints on her arms, insisting she fell down the stairs. I picture her saying all of it. The classic abuse victim responses delivered with practiced conviction.

Nick speaks from behind her, his voice low and controlled. "There were reports," he says. "Teachers noticed, but no one else cared to do anything."

Bevin nods. "They said that I was exaggerating. A lying for attention teenager." Her eyes harden slightly.

Then she reaches into her pocket.

"I kept proof," she says.

Her phone trembles in her hand as she unlocks it. For a second she just stares at the screen, like she might change her mind. Then she turns it toward me.

"I didn't think anyone would believe me without it."

The video starts playing.

It's shaky, filmed from low down like the phone's half-hidden. I can hear an angry man's voice.

Her dad.

Even through the tiny speaker, the rage in it makes my skin crawl.

The camera jerks, like she's trying to hide it. A door slams open so hard that it echoes. He storms into the frame, his face red, his movements fast and jerky. He's yelling at her, and then the video lurches violently as if she's being grabbed.

Bevin flinches beside me.

The screen fills with blurred motion. The sound of something hitting the floor. Then the video cuts off.

The room falls dead silent. Karrie and I look at each other in shock.

Bevin swipes to the next thing before I can say anything.

Pictures.

A dozen pictures with bruises all over her body.

I knew her father was involved. My gut never lets me down.

A sick feeling spreads through my stomach. The journal. The missing page was about him, just as I thought. The things her dad said in the store.

Nick continues, like he's filling in the spaces she can't. "By the time I met her, she was already in survival mode. Always waiting for something bad to happen. Home wasn't safe for her. No one was stepping in to help."

He pauses.

"I didn't plan it," he says. "Not at first. I just listened, and tried to help. But it kept getting worse." He exhales slowly. "If she stayed there, she wasn't going to make it out okay."

Bevin's voice drops quieter. "The last night was bad," she says. "Worse than usual. I remember thinking that if I didn't leave, I was going to die there."

Her words stab at my heart.

I believe her.

That's the part that scares me the most.

Nick shifts slightly, leaning his shoulder against the wall. "She wasn't the only one," he says. "The others here... it was the same thing. Different houses, different people, same story. Abuse. Neglect. You name it."

Karrie inhales sharply beside me.

"They came from bad homes," Nick continues. "Homes they couldn't escape on their own. Some of them tried going through the system first." His jaw tightens. "It didn't work."

"So you helped them disappear," I say.

It's not really a question. It's exactly what he is telling me.

Nick nods once. "I helped them get out."

Bevin looks up at me with eyes that have seen too much, her chapped lips pressed into a determined line. "He didn't kidnap me," she confesses, her voice steadier now. "Leaving was what I wanted. I begged him."

It's still kidnapping when it involves a minor. An adult cannot take a child somewhere without the guardian's permission, even if that child is the one pushing for it.

I think about the missing posters... her face plastered across telephone poles, taped to storefront windows, fluttering in the rain. The desperate searches through woods and abandoned buildings, volunteers with flashlights calling her name into the darkness. Her parents crying on the news.

What her dad said in that grocery store aisle. *"Some people just run off."*

Nick continues quietly. "They all have new names now. New lives. No one here knows anyone else's real name. That's intentional. It keeps them safe, even from each other."

I look around the room. Evidence of a life that kept going while we all thought she was dead.

"They've had therapy," Nick says. "They're working. Building lives. Healing."

Healing.

The word sits heavy in my chest.

I look back at Bevin and really look at her. She looks older but healthy.

Alive in a way she might not have been otherwise.

This is a twist I never expected. And for the first time, I don't know what the right answer is anymore.

CHAPTER 30

CALEB

Bevin's eyes lock on mine, wide and desperate.

"Please, Detective Reed," she pleads, her voice breaking into jagged fragments. "You can't tell anyone."

Nick stands beside her. I can see the tension in his jaw.

"You don't understand," Bevin continues. "My family... they're okay now. They've moved on. They're at peace with me being gone."

Her hands tremble as she wipes at her eyes.

"And I love it here," she admits. "I love my life. So do the others. Some even have apartments, jobs... real lives. Good lives."

She shakes her head hard.

"If you report this, you'll ruin everything," she pleads.

I swallow down a lump, my throat constricting as if I've swallowed sand. The more she pleads, the more twisting I feel in my gut. "Bevin... you're still a missing person."

"So are they," she says quickly. "But they're safe."

"What I'm doing is helping them," Nick pleads.

"You understand what this looks like?" I state. "You taking in underage kids? Giving them new names? Making them disappear?"

His expression doesn't change. "I know exactly what it looks like."

I hesitate before speaking again, tasting the accusation before letting it free.

"That picture," I bring up, pointing to my phone. "The one of you and Bevin. It looked like you were dating."

Bevin's head snaps up. "We weren't."

Nick shakes his head immediately, palms raised like a surrender. "It was an act."

My stomach quivers like I've swallowed a fistful of moths.

"For who?" I probe.

"Anyone who might come looking," Nick says. "It's easier if people assume we were close; then it wouldn't seem like a red flag if they saw her with me around the time she went missing."

Bevin nods. "He never touched me. Not like that."

Nick's voice is firm now. "I have never done anything

inappropriate with any of them. I swear."

I do not know why, but I believe him. The way both of their eyes are looking at me when they are saying these things. Nick and Bevin are telling the truth. I can feel it in my gut.

Bevin steps closer to me. "Please," she whispers. "Just pretend you never saw us."

Her voice cracks when she says the last word.

"You found me. You know I'm okay. Isn't that enough?" she bargains.

I don't have an answer to that. My training and my humanity are at war within me.

Nothing makes this morally right. The thought of these kids being missed by people, presumed dead, and yet here they are, just fine. But then again, different circumstances, this is kind of what it was like with Lee. We were that family, and he was perfectly fine living another life.

I tell them I will think on it. I won't do anything at this moment; that much I can assure them. Nick and I swapped numbers to keep in touch. Cassidy and Nova waited for us long enough, probably wondering if we'd fallen into some backwoods trap. Karrie and I say our goodbyes and head out to the car.

The highway stretches endlessly in front of us. Rain taps

steadily against the windshield, the wipers sweeping back and forth in a slow, hypnotic rhythm. Of course, it's still raining. It's like the sky itself is weeping with indecision.

The house, the stories, the truth about Nick... it all feels like a dream now, fading at the edges like an old photograph. But it's real.

"I think this was the right choice," Cassidy says beside me. "Leaving it. Letting them stay safe. No one needs to know."

I nod, staring out at the never-ending highway. "Yeah... maybe." But even as I say it, my heart cringes, folding in on itself like origami made of flesh.

I catch Karrie's reflection in the rearview mirror, her face half-shadowed by the setting sun streaming through the rear window. "Thank you for coming forward."

She glances back at me, lifting her eyebrows in surprise. "You're welcome."

I hold her gaze in the mirror, noting the dark circles under her eyes. "Bevin's parents were possible suspects at first, but I never actually believed they'd do these things to her. It makes the dad's behavior make more sense now."

Karrie nods, her fingers fidgeting with her phone. "Yeah... wow. Honestly, I thought Nick did something bad to her. I never expected him to be helping her."

"I don't think I ever had a case turn out like this, now that I think of it," I admit, my voice sounding rough even to my own ears. "A tough decision lies ahead."

"You aren't going to report this, are you?" Nova asks.

"I might have to eventually," I respond, my knuckles whitening as I grip the steering wheel tighter.

"We will all get into trouble. You aren't even on duty. Cassidy broke into that guy's..." Nova's voice rises with each word.

"I know. Trust me, I know. All of this is like on repeat in my mind," I interrupt, the words scraping my throat.

Families are still waiting in living rooms with faded photos and untouched bedrooms.

Not necessarily good families. But loved ones nonetheless, checking their phones for news that I now know the answers to.

Somewhere out there are grandparents, siblings, aunts... people who never hurt them. People who still wonder. Still waiting and hoping. Ones who may not even know what twisted things the parents were doing behind drawn curtains. Those people deserve more than the hollow ache of uncertainty.

Cassidy sets her hand on my arm. "What do we do about

Anderson?"

Nova sighs. "Call her. Explain what happened. Tell her to drop it."

Drop it.

Like it's nothing.

Like it's not evidence.

Like it's not a crime that has left scars on everyone it touched.

"I will deal with Anderson," I say, my voice steadier than my conscience.

"None of this ever happened," Cassidy reminds me, her eyes darting to the rearview mirror as if someone might be following us.

I glance at Karrie again; her face relaxed now, a quiet satisfaction in her eyes.

I should finally be able to rest, knowing that I have solved the case that has haunted me. That should fill the hollow space inside me. But it doesn't.

My badge is still sitting in my desk drawer at home. I wasn't even supposed to be within ten miles of this case file. If anyone discovers I know... they could charge me with obstruction of justice, misconduct, and accessory after the fact.

My career would collapse like a house of cards. I'd go to

prison.

Hell, Cassidy could spend years in a cell for breaking and entering.

Fuck! My stomach churns and twists as if I've swallowed broken glass just thinking about it.

I stare out the window. The rain has softened to a silver mist that catches the sunlight, almost cleansing in its gentle persistence.

I picture Bevin saying, *"Please pretend you never saw me."*

Images of the bruises, the video, and her father's voice flood my mind. Then I picture the years of searching for her. The teachers, friends, and families.

Waiting.

Not all of them are monsters with secrets to hide. Some are people with hearts that break a little more each year. People who will die never knowing what happened to the girl they loved.

Turning it in could destroy the lives those kids have built. Not turning it in could destroy mine in one swift collapse.

As I drive on, the weight settles heavier on my chest with every passing mile. This isn't over. Deep down, I haven't decided what I'm going to do.

CHAPTER 31

CALEB

THREE WEEKS LATER

The house thrums with life. Carter streaks through the living room in frantic circles, his laughter echoing off the walls. I can't believe how big he has gotten. It feels like the last time I saw him he was wobbling from the couch to the coffee table, arms out for balance. Now he moves like a missile, cutting sharp corners as if he's been training for it.

Lexy adjusts the blue cap on one twin while I'm balanced on the edge of the couch cushion, holding the other twin as she hiccups against my chest every few seconds. She's so small it feels like I'm holding something breakable. Her tiny fingers curl and uncurl against my shirt.

In the doorway to the kitchen, Mom stands framed by warm lamplight, a shiny spatula in one hand and her apron dusted with flour. "Careful," she calls with a teasing lilt, "or you'll have twins chasing you next!" She laughs, passing a plate of snacks to my sister. My father is chuckling in the corner at her words.

It's a perfect moment.

I take a deep breath, watching my family together, and feel that rare, calm sense of rightness. This is life.

My life.

The doorbell's chime cuts through it all. Carter freezes mid-lap, head swiveling toward the sound. I nestle the baby into the cushioned bassinet, and I step over scattered blocks and duck under the hanging garland of streamers, heading for the door. A plastic truck digs into the bottom of my foot, and I wince, nudging it aside with my heel.

Merrick is standing outside the door, a crooked smile breaking across his face. "Thought you might be growing roots in there by now."

"Not quite yet." I pull him in with a quick shoulder grip. "Let's get some air."

For a second, I just look at him. It hits me. I no longer feel the immense guilt when I see his face. I guess the therapy has been helping after all.

We slip into the backyard, where the late afternoon sun drapes golden light over the lawn. The air hangs thick and hot. The kind of heat that presses against your skin and makes your shirt cling to your back.

Merrick's hand lands heavy between my shoulder blades. "So... you planning on coming back?"

I feel excitement pulse behind my ribs. "Funny you should ask. I've been thinking about it for the last few days. I'm ready."

The words come out easier than I expect.

His face cracks with relief. "It's been dull without you. The last case I worked was another missing child. Turns out it was just a bid for attention. A money scam by the parents." He shakes his head, a rueful smile tugging at his lips. "Some people, man."

"Jesus," I mutter, tilting my face to the blistering sky. "Some sick world we live in."

He rams his shoulder into mine. "I missed you, man."

My throat tightens. "Missed you too."

We stroll back to the house, where golden light spills onto the porch. Through the window, I see Carter hugging Dad's leg. Merrick watches the scene with a smirk. "So... married yet?"

I laugh, glancing over my shoulder. "Not yet. Five weeks to go."

Merrick's eyes light up. His grin turns predatory. "I still get bachelor party duty, right?"

I chuckle to myself. "Of course. Don't even ask."

He flashes a triumphant grin. "I apologize for the shit that may go down ahead of time."

"God help me," I mutter, already dreading it. I fix him with a steel glare that would make suspects confess. Then break it with a smirk.

He laughs.

I lock my arm around his neck in a half-headlock, and say, "Alright... come on. Time to meet my brother."

My hand lingers on the doorknob for just a second before I turn it.

Carter barrels toward me like I've been gone for years instead of minutes. I catch him before he collides with my legs, lifting him easily, his laughter bursting against my ear.

The door swings shut behind us with a soft click.

I guide Merrick toward the kitchen where Lee is standing with Lexy, holding baby Dustin.

"Lee," I say, "this is Merrick. One of my work partners. Merrick, this is my brother, Lee."

Lee shifts the baby gently and offers his free hand. "I've heard a lot about you."

Merrick shakes it with an easy smile. "Probably not as much as I've heard about you."

Lee laughs. "Fair enough."

Merrick studies him for a second, then smirks. "I definitely see the resemblance."

Lee smiles at that, introducing him to Lexy. Cassidy steps up beside me, her shoulder brushing mine.

Nicole is saying something rapid-fire to her, gesturing dramatically with one of the twins' tiny socks in her hand.

Cassidy leans into me, slipping her arm around my waist. "Nicole is grilling me about the wedding," she murmurs.

I snort. "That's what sisters-in-law are for, right?"

Cassidy shakes her head and chuckles.

I stand back and take it all in for a moment.

Merrick and Lee are already deep in conversation, Merrick gesturing with animated hands while Lee laughs... a genuine laugh, the kind that comes from the chest. They look as if they've known each other for years.

An image overlaps reality in my mind.

Bevin laughing with Nick.

He's beside her, watching her the way people watch something they worked hard to protect.

I exhale slowly.

I made the right choice leaving them be.

Why ruin a good thing just to satisfy a report? Why drag someone back to a place that broke them just because the paperwork says you should?

Some endings don't look the way people expect them to.

Some people aren't meant to be found.

CHAPTER 32

EPILOGUE

THREE MONTHS LATER

Rain hammers the windshield like thrown gravel, turning the road into a black mirror. Adams' cruiser bleeds red light ahead of me, the taillights smearing across the wet asphalt. I grip the wheel until my knuckles ache, trying to steady my breathing as my chest constricts.

I hate driving in the rain. Especially somewhere in a rush.

The radio murmurs quietly, background noise more than anything. My eyes stay fixed on her taillights.

I think back to the phone conversation we just had. Shantelle's words still ring in my ears. Her voice was a tone I never heard before.

"Reed, I know who it is. I know who the killer is," she blurted out.

I asked her who, but she responded with, "Just follow me.

It's hard to explain. I don't know his name, but I know where he lives."

Now I'm chasing her through this storm, my heart slamming against my ribs to the point of causing a heart attack. After weeks of dead ends and body bags, we're finally closing in on the Zip-Tie killer.

I press the gas, closing the distance between us. My headlights spill over the back of her cruiser, reflecting in long streaks across the wet road. She turns onto a wider street lined with warehouses and chain-link fences. The streetlights are too far apart out here, leaving long stretches of shadow between them.

The hair on the back of my neck rises. Something is wrong.

Adams slows slightly as she approaches the intersection ahead. Headlights burst into view from the right. Coming too fast. Way too fast.

A massive loading truck barrels through the intersection without stopping.

"Adams!" I shout, even though I know she can't hear me.

The truck smashes into the cruiser's side with a sickening screech of metal. The collision snaps like a rifle shot, rattling my chest. My ears pound from the blast. Her cruiser launches skyward as if catapulted.

HOLY FUCK!

It's like I'm watching in slow motion as her car flips through the air and rolls twice.

Glass sprays through the air, catching the streetlight like falling ice.

The cruiser slams roof-first into concrete, metal crumpling like paper, and skids in a blinding spray of white-hot sparks before jerking to a dead stop.

I stomp the brake so hard my ankle burns. My car whips sideways, fishtailing before stopping crooked across the road.

For a second, there's nothing. No sound except the ticking of my engine and the hiss of rain hitting hot metal.

I throw the door open and run.

"Adams!" I yell.

My boots hammer through puddles, splashing water up my legs as I sprint toward the mangled wreckage. The cruiser is crushed inward, the roof flattened, the windows shattered. This isn't good at all.

"Oh my God, SHANTELLE!" Her name rips from my throat.

Then I see movement. Across the street. A man in dark clothes, his hood up, running from the truck that hit her. Running as if he had planned this.

My heart lurches into my throat.

That's him.

That's fucking him.

He vanishes behind a tree.

If I move now, I can end this. End him.

He reappears, darting toward the warehouse alley.

I take a step after him. Then another. The distance between us is growing.

A sound stops me. A weak, broken groan.

Behind me.

Adams' cruiser lies crushed like a beer can in the middle of the road. Black smoke belches from the crumpled hood.

Oh fuck! That car's gonna blow. I need to get her out now.

I stand there for half a second that feels like forever.

Him.

Or her.

The man melts into the darkness.

"DAMN IT!" I scream, already sprinting back.

I run to the cruiser and fall to my knees beside it.

"Shantelle, stay with me!"

She's hanging upside down in the seatbelt, her hair dangling toward the crushed roof. Blood cascades down her face in rivulets, spattering onto the roof with a sickening patter.

Shit. That's too much blood. I need to stop the bleeding. My hands convulse as I thrust them through jagged glass. Shards slice into my knees.

"Hey," I say, my voice coming out ragged. "Hey, you're going to be okay."

She doesn't move. Her eyes are closed. I touch her shoulder. "Wake up..."

Nothing.

My fingers come away wet when I reach higher. My hand is now full of her blood.

"Oh, shit!"

I grab my radio and call it in.

"Officer down!" I shout. "Officer down! Major collision at Halbrook and 9th! Suspect fled on foot! I need backup and EMS *now!*"

Static crackles.

"Units en route."

I drop the radio and press both hands against the worst of the bleeding, trying to figure out where it's coming from.

"No, no, no..." I gasp.

Rain mixes with the blood running down my wrists.

"You're okay," I beg, even though my voice is shaking. "You're okay. Stay with me."

Gasoline reek chokes the air. The car's going to become a fireball any second. I need to get her out.

Her head lolls slightly, completely limp. Panic claws its way up my throat as I try to unbuckle her to pull her out of the vehicle. The seatbelt won't budge.

"COME ON!" I scream in her face.

Sirens wail faintly in the distance. Still too far away. I press harder on the wound.

Her chest is barely moving now. Each breath is a gamble.

"Listen to me," I gasp, my voice cracking as I fight to keep control. "You said you knew who it was. You have to tell me. Please... wake up and tell me."

Thunder rumbles overhead, shaking the air.

I lean my forehead briefly against the crushed frame of the car.

"Fuck, Shantelle," I shout. "Don't you die on me."

I have no way of knowing if she can hear me. All I know for sure is the bastard who did this is getting away.

AFTERWORD

Did you enjoy reading *One Twisted Game?*

If you did, I would really appreciate it if you could leave a review on Amazon. Your feedback means the world to me! If it wasn't your cup of tea, that's okay too—I still want to thank you for giving it a chance and for taking the time to check it out. Your support means a lot!

Also, feel free to check out my website, where you can easily access my other books and stay updated on future releases. Thank you for your support!

https://jessicalynnscreations.com

ALSO

BY JESSICA LYNN SORENSEN

Jamie Smith wakes up after a wild party with no memory of the night before—only to discover a body in the trunk of her car. The victim? Her ex-boyfriend's new girlfriend. As Jamie's mind spirals into confusion and paranoia, she struggles with one terrifying question: Did she commit murder, or is someone setting her up?

As the story flips between her present-day horror and flashbacks to the night of the party, Jamie is forced to confront hidden truths, betrayals, and the possibility that someone is manipulating her every move. In this twisted psychological thriller, nothing is as it seems, and the closer Jamie gets to the truth, the more dangerous her situation becomes. **(Secrets After Sunset)**

When Zyler Dixon moves into an estate sale-furnished house to start anew, he never expected his life to take a spine-chilling turn. The first morning in his new home, he wakes up to a woman in his bed—the same woman the realtor claimed to be dead. Shocked, Zyler confronts her, only to be met with an emotional revelation: the woman insists he is her husband and has been missing for two years. **(Home Sweet Hostage)**

When Detective Caleb Reed spots a distraught young woman on a desolate highway, he knows he can't just drive by. She has no memory of who she is or how she ended up cold, weak, and hungry in an abandoned shed. Driven by his unresolved guilt over his missing brother and a relentless hero complex, Caleb takes her in, determined to help her discover her identity. But in his rush to protect her, he may have made a critical mistake—not involving law enforcement. **(A Stranger Within: First book**

in the detective caleb reed series)

Detective Caleb Reed's latest case seems straightforward at first: missing four-year-old girl, Bailey Moore. But things take a **wicked** turn when the parents give two very different stories. The mother insists her daughter disappeared last night, while the father claims she tragically died months ago in a car accident.

As Caleb digs deeper, he finds himself caught between two conflicting realities, unsure who—or what—to believe. This case might not be his most high-profile or challenging on the surface, but it's shaping up to be one of his most **bizarre** ones.

*Someone has to be lying.*But who—and how far are they willing to go to keep the truth hidden? **(Whispering Rain: Second book in the Detective Caleb Reed Series)**

Secrets linger like shadows in Joplin, Missouri, where the sins of *infidelity* have a deadly consequence. When a serial killer terrorizes the town, preying on those who break their vows, one woman manages to escape, aiding in the *capture* of this ruthless killer. But when new threats start appearing and her abusive ex resurfaces from the dead, Angela's world spirals into a web of deceit. **(Echoes Of The Hunted)**

ABOUT THE AUTHOR

Jessica was born in the heart of South Carolina. She experienced an unique childhood, with a few tragedies that shaped her perspective and fueled her creative spirit.

After her father's untimely passing, and her mother's subsequent remarriage, she moved to Canada as a young child. Amidst the constant flux, her unwavering passion for writing and storytelling emerged as a stable companion, providing stability throughout the years.

She is a mother of four boys. Due to circumstances, she was unable to return to work outside of the home after the birth of her twins. Sparking her interest to become an author.

Dive into more of her gripping tales with "Echoes Of The Hunted" and "A Stranger Within." Don't miss out on these captivating reads!

www.ingramcontent.com/pod-product-compliance
Lightning Source LLC
LaVergne TN
LVHW091050080826
845145LV00002B/686

* 9 7 8 1 0 6 9 3 8 6 1 7 5 *